SO-DUV-496

THE DISSEMBLERS

THE DISSEMBLERS

LIZA CAMPBELL

THE PERMANENT PRESS
Sag Harbor, NY 11963

For information, address:
    The Permanent Press
    4170 Noyac Road
    Sag Harbor, NY 11963
    www.thepermanentpress.com

Library of Congress Cataloging-in-Publication Data

Campbell, Liza–
    The dissemblers / Liza Campbell.
        p. cm.
    ISBN 978-1-57962-205-3 (hardcover : alk. paper)
        1. Women painters—Fiction. 2. Art—Forgeries—Fiction.
    3. Santa Fe (N.M.)—Fiction. 4. Isolation (Philosophy)—Fiction.
    5. Identity (Psychology)—Fiction. 6. Psychological fiction.
    I. Title.

PS3603.A4773D57 2010
813'.6—dc22   2010017938

Printed in the United States of America.

PROLOGUE

I never met Georgia O'Keeffe. I was born on the day that she died, so our lifespans overlap only by a few hours. I like to think of those hours of coexistence as refracted in a slightly different shade than the preceding or following years, as when a yellow circle and a red circle overlap in an orange sliver.

I never met Georgia, but I think we would have been great friends. She doesn't smile in her photos, at least not with her teeth. Her smiles are close-lipped and secretive. She looks at the camera as if she is challenging the photographer. Her lower lip is slightly thinner than the upper, and her nose is strong and uncompromising. She has a square jaw and eyes that look past the camera and past the photographer. She looks at me and then through me disinterestedly. Thinking of something very far away from me. She is not thinking about the photographer, he only happens to be there, neither an inconvenience nor a pleasure.

I never met Georgia, but I've studied her paintings with an intensity that could recall the dead. What I love about her work is the aloneness. They are paintings that render our human lives insignificant, paintings of stone, mountain, sky. I imagine the act of her painting was both a recognition of and a rebellion against her own tininess. I wonder if she walked around always with the knowledge of how fleeting her body was, and if this scared her.

One day in 1929, Georgia stepped from a train in New Mexico and the first thing she saw was the sky. Constant

5

and cloudless, the sky in New Mexico reaches all the way down to the mountains. It wanted to swallow her, that sky. Her friend walked out in front, but Georgia, *my* Georgia, stood back a little, looking at the cottonwoods. Three cottonwoods on the other side of the packed dirt road, their leaves just beginning to uncurl. Sticky leaves, born the color of inchworms. The station was pink and made of mud. When the train whistled and clacked and roared away, the wind it left behind was dry, smelled of sunshine and dry dirt. Leaving the train station in a Ford Model A, Georgia sat in the backseat. She leaned over to the man who was driving, and shouted over the noise of the engine and the wind. *Teach me how to drive*, she said. *I'm going to learn to drive.*

PART I

*"I find that I have painted my life—
things happening in my life—
without knowing."*

—GEORGIA O'KEEFFE

1

To begin a forgery:

Study the painting. Be obsessive. Bring your nose close enough to smell the painting. Close enough that you forget the names of colors. Imagine the paint particle by particle. Cross your eyes. Look for brushstrokes. Look for which color was placed first, how fat the brush was, whether one layer dried before the next was placed. Then walk to the other side of the room. Squint your eyes. Find the darkest corner of the canvas, then the lightest place. Unlearn the object of the painting. If you are making a forgery of a painting of a bone, forget what bone is. Remember the parts of the painting that are not bone. Turn the painting upside down.

Remember the first drawing class you ever took. The metal folding chair in the center of a circle of students, as if waiting for an accused man, as if all the faces behind drawing pads were demanding alibis from an invisible witness. Your teacher said, *don't draw the chair. Draw the space around the chair.* And you were bewildered.

I've always assumed I would be successful. Perhaps this is a common fallacy. All piano players imagine themselves as soloists at Carnegie Hall, and every kid on a baseball team imagines himself in the major leagues. This is perhaps the nature of youth, and the cruelty of aging is in the ways we become distracted and learn that this glory is not for us. We move to low-ceilinged apartments with no piano, we leave our baseball mitts in the bottom of the closet with dust thick as paint, we get jobs at firms and banks—and then we are adults. But not me.

That bit about all piano players imagining themselves as soloists, I don't know if that's true. I don't know if everyone, like me, carries with them always the unfulfilled sense of being destined for greater things. Maybe this is simply arrogance. Omar had it, too, this nagging sense of unattained greatness. I would watch him working sometimes in the café; and when the line died down or he was cleaning the espresso machines, I would see his movements slow and become repetitive, and he would step outside of himself. I could see him weighing his two lives, the one he was actually living against that glorious one he was supposed to live, but had somehow missed.

I like the precision of forgery. The absolute concentration of copying a line, or a shade. The paintings that I copied, I understood. I owned them. At first I didn't think of them as forgeries. They were exercises. Although to call them that belittles the absolute peace I found in making them. They were not exercises in the sense of a school child repeating multiplication tables, but the exercises of a monk who sits without moving, intoning the same three syllables over and over.

Remember the first drawing class. A room with floor to ceiling windows, all the students oblivious to one another, all looking to the center, to the space around the chair. And perhaps you could only see the chair, but not the space. Perhaps you were stuck on the essence of *chair*, the emptiness and waiting. I dream sometimes about that chair. In my dream I am sitting in the middle of that circle. All the students examine me with penetrating eyes, and they don't draw me, but all the things about me that I will never say aloud. Things like:

If I were in a crowded room when a fire broke out, I don't know if I would try and save anyone but myself.

Love scares me.

I'm smarter than everyone I know.

2

If I were to start at the beginning, I would tell the circle of strangers that I grew up in Boston, where I had a traditionally happy childhood divided cheerfully into four distinct seasons each year. My parents were both professors, theology and geology, which are not as different as one may think. On weekends we would drive to the country, or so I called it, tame and billboard-free, to pick apples or hike. (*Glacial rocks*, my mother would point out. *A Bhikkhu's cave*, my father would say.) Summers were spent contemplating the placid Massachusetts Atlantic or the more temperamental Maine coastline with my eccentric lobster-fishing uncle.

An artist friend of my parents once said that one does not learn to draw, but learns to see. Her name, incidentally, was Bunny, and she had the amazing ability to change her voice and imitate virtually anybody. She was extremely opinionated. I've always been in awe of extremely opinionated people. Perhaps that's why, later, I was drawn to Maya. It reveals a kind of confidence, to hold so fiercely to a belief. Me, I'm always questioning. And when I do believe something, I'm still not extremely opinionated because I can't help but think how small and unimportant I am, after all. That's what intellectual parents will do to you. Try looking at your life from the perspective of geological time. Or as the reincarnation of a millipede. Bunny was evidently unfazed by the billions of eons of swirling dust that preceded her, and would say with conviction that Jackson Pollock was a genius and Andy Warhol a contemptible fraud, and her students would absolutely respect her, if not agree with her.

An only child, I learned the language of adults at a young age, and Bunny's conviction made an impression on me. So when Bunny spoke of learning to see, I began to look. I realized that objects and people were not jumbles of intersecting lines, but a collection of light and shadows. And the world was suddenly astounding. Even now, walking through Santa Fe, I am struck dumb by the slant of the afternoon sun on a brick building. Speaking with strangers, I forget to listen to their words, distracted by the light playing on the changing planes of their expressions. I'm not sure if this way of seeing is a blessing or a curse.

Omar used to catch me slipping into these reveries. *Ivy, where are you?* he'd sing. *Come back to me.* Taking my chin in his hand.

When I announced at the age of eleven that I was going to be an artist, my parents were noncommitally supportive; and six years later, they stoically watched their only child pack crates and suitcases into a secondhand Corolla and depart for art school in Chicago. Then, having successfully reared a child and seen her off, they returned happily to tectonic plates and Eastern sutras.

In art school, I learned nothing much of use except patience as I sketched my way through eighty-seven boxes of charcoal. We talked about art in words like *post-structural, cyber-industrial, post-Freudo-Lacanian.* Teachers built philosophies from coat hangers and students carved worlds from balls of Gouda cheese wax.

The first of Georgia's paintings that I ever really looked at—*really* looked at, not just passed in a museum and made a half-hearted identification of flower, bone—was in Chicago, one particularly bleak January day when I hadn't seen the sun for months. It was a winter painting, a raven flying over white snowy hills. The whole painting had only three colors: white for the hills, an undulating black V for the bird, and

12

the blue sky. It was not a painting of a bird, but a painting of the sky that happened to be shaped around a lone black bird. After five semesters of theories and analysis and symbolism, the painting struck me. It seemed so . . . pure. It didn't scream any ideas to me, it was simply there, shapes rendered on canvas that made me want to look.

Georgia spent a year at art school in Chicago, the same school that I attended. Later she lived there and worked as an illustrator. I know she hated it, because I hated it too, especially in the winters. It's crowded, and at the beginning of the century I imagine the air was smoky, unbreathable. Smoke escaping from tall industrial smokestacks and blending into an iron-grey sky. Georgia did freelance drawing for advertising, and she hated it. She hated drawing intricate lace and the embroidery on dresses, she hated drawing for a deadline, she hated the daily newspapers that churned out copies of her ads. Sharp-smelling, smudging newspaper ink. She did this for two years, and what she hated most of all was that she had quit painting. But it would have killed her to pick up a brush, she would have dissolved into tears. She was stubborn, my Georgia, and if she couldn't devote herself wholly to painting, then she wouldn't do it at all.

For these years, she was the ex-piano playing banker, the baseball player with the untouched dusty mitt; and these were the worst, the hardest years of her life, because she'd given up on the thing she wanted most. I think that when you give up on the thing you want most, you get a little closer to your death, because your life isn't as important to you anymore.

When I finished school, I followed Georgia to New Mexico. I moved to Santa Fe and found an apartment east of the plaza, upstairs from a string-instrument repair shop run by a white-haired man of indeterminate age named Rich. The hours of the shop were as erratic as Rich's moods. Sometimes weeks would go by without his old white station wagon crunching into the gravel driveway. Sometimes

13

I would wake up in the middle of the night and see a square of light spilling from his window into our tiny yard. There was one other apartment above my own, and a tiny window-less stairwell with worn carpeting from the ground to the top floor.

It was late summer when I moved. As the days short-ened, I learned the tilts of shadow on adobe at different hours of the day. I bought a Siamese fighting fish and named him Russell. I invented names for the two neighborhood cats that haunted and hunted the alley, leaping three feet to top garbage cans effortlessly, snaky tails twitching into question marks. I grew accustomed to the particular hum of the old refrigerator, and stopped rolling over in sleep when it switched on and off at night.

I lived nearly a month in my apartment without meeting my neighbors upstairs. I hadn't seen them, but I grew accustomed to their life-noises. Footsteps passing over my kitchen, treading above my living room, flushing the toilet above my bathroom. In the afternoons, the sounds of string instruments being tuned, and the same scales and passages starting, stopping, restarting abruptly. I identified a cello and a violin. Sometimes they played music I recognized, Mozart, Bach. But more often they played in fitful measures that I didn't recognize. At seven o'clock, cooking smells would begin to wander through invisible cracks in my ceiling, onions in olive oil, garlic and ginger, blackened peppers. And in the mornings, the sounds of their love-making in the bed above my own.

At the Georgia O'Keeffe Museum, I applied for a job as a security guard so I could spend all day with the paint-ings. Instead I was put in the gift shop. *You have such a nice open face,* said Aline, my manager. She wore knee-length skirts that impeccably matched her shoes. *Great for retail.* So I sold date books and paperweights and dangling glass ear-rings. The security guards walked by, unsmiling, all of them

14

heavily tattooed and dark-haired and not, I thought, particularly interested in the paintings.

The O'Keeffe museum architecture is spare, all skylights and concrete floors. The doors are so tall that the architect must have intended everyone who enters to feel like a dwarf. When my shift ended I would spend time in the gallery. I studied a different painting each day.

My life in Santa Fe was solitary. I didn't eschew company, but neither did I seek it out. Sometimes after work I would go out for drinks with Kate, the heavy-lidded girl who worked at the front desk of the museum. I small-talked art and politics with her friends. Sometimes, but not often, I small-talked my painting when the inquiries were genuine. But more often, I walked alone to my dark spare room to heat a can of soup before I sat in front of the easel. Which I did, nearly every night, with a determination not unlike stubbornness. Some nights the hours dissolved in the space between brushstrokes, nights turned to cobalt and swollen reds, the final rendering of the shadow beneath a shoulder blade. And some nights I hated, and touched the canvas only once and regretted colors. Outside, the tomcats swam in and out of streetlight pools.

When you stop painting, the hardest thing in the world is to start again. This is why painters become compulsive about their routine. Missing one day may not paralyze you, but if you miss a week you are terrified that you will never paint again. In school, there are endless assignments and deadlines that keep you working, even if you don't like what you're doing. On your own, where nobody cares if you paint or not, you have to give yourself assignments. This is how I did the painting that started everything.

It was one of Georgia's paintings that I hadn't seen before working at the museum. A flower, jack-in-the-pulpit, that looked like a ripped seam. The lucid light in the center of the flower made me feel as though I were looking through a tear into the brightness associated with dying. I took a

15

poster print of the painting from the gift shop and leaned it next to my own canvas.

I gave myself an assignment, to imitate the painting. We would do this in school sometimes, to learn treatments of color and line that weren't our own. I'd always been good at it. With most students, you look at their imitations, their paintings in the style of such-and-such, and you can see the particular vision of the student. Much in the same way that eighteen paintings of the same vase and violin will look like eighteen different paintings. But my paintings always seemed to be devoid of my personality. When I say that my imitations were always the best in the class, I don't say this to brag; I only mean that they most resembled the original. I don't even say this with particular pride, because I'm not sure if this total erasure of self is something to be proud of.

So I worked on Georgia's *Jack-in-the-Pulpit* series. Even though it was a small flower, it was like painting a landscape. The stamen a waterfall, petals like smooth canyon walls.

When Georgia was twenty-seven-years old, she said she was tired of painting as she had been taught, painting as other people painted. She said that she had things in her head that were unlike anything she had seen, and that was what she wanted to draw. So she put away all her paints, she put away color. She spread her floor with cheap newsprint, and night after night she knelt with charcoal and drew what she wanted to draw. Lines and circles and angles and shadows.

16

3

I met Jake first.

One afternoon after the museum had closed I stood
before a large black and white portrait of Georgia that
hangs in the front gallery. The glass reflected my face over
Georgia's. Track lighting overhead cast deep shadows in
my eyesockets from which my nose protruded like a beak.
Georgia must have been in her nineties when the picture
was taken. She looks nun-like, beatific, dressed all in loose
black with a scarf over her head. She is not looking directly
at the camera, but at an angle. She looks like Mother Teresa.
Peaceful. I wonder if as we get older we grow into solitude,
or just become accustomed to it.

I noticed one of the guards standing behind me then.
Like all the museum guards, he wore a white collared shirt
with flaps of fabric on the shoulders that buttoned to make
loops, like the shirts that policemen wear. He had an earpiece
and even a silver badge pinned to his right breast pocket
that I couldn't read, but knew said SECURITY. The wrists of
his guard shirt were unbuttoned and I could see the snaking
end of a tattoo on his wrist. His hair was a little longer than
would be considered professional, and stood up from his head
like a bird ruffling its feathers. He had a carefully clipped
beard and eyebrows so thick they almost met in the middle in
a single dark slash. Unlike mine, his eyes shone in the track
lighting, reflecting the bright pinpoints from the ceiling. He
was looking directly at me. I waited for him to speak, but he
didn't. He stood with good, straight posture, as if supported

by a strong and confident spine. Though I didn't yet know his name, I'd noticed him before, patrolling the rooms. He struck me as one of those individuals who looks outwards instead of inwards. One of the few who don't worry about how they appear to others—they assume they will be liked, and thus, easily, are liked. Unlike the men I'd gone to school with, all of them consumed with their own ideas, taking the world in and guarding it closely, Jake projected his world outward in a way that private people marvel at.

We stood, my back to him, but looking at one another in the mirror of Georgia's portrait until it became awkward and the silent museum bristled around us. We looked at each other until it was past awkward, and his reflection began to smile above Georgia's scarved head, starting with the corners of his mouth. Finally I dropped his gaze and turned.

"I win," he said.

This is how I met Jake and how I still think of him, tall and firm-jawed and seemingly without a care.

"I think we're neighbors," he said. "Camino de Flores? Above the string shop. My girlfriend and I live on the top floor."

"Are you the violin or the cello?" I asked.

"Guess," he said.

"Cello," I said.

"Violin," he said. Then he added, "My grandpa taught me to play."

When I knew Jake better, he would tell me that he started playing music only because he wanted applause. And when I knew him better than that, he would tell me that he was deaf in his right ear and only heard half the applause. And when I knew him better than that, I would kiss all my secrets into that deaf ear with the tiniest of whispers.

Maya was the cello player and Jake's girlfriend, and she was shorter than I'd thought from her footsteps above me. One

18

of those short people who make tall people feel awkward. She wore long skirts and tall boots and had unruly hair. She always seemed to be jingling. Tinkling earrings, chiming bracelets. I came to associate the sound with her very being, and imagined that even when she was naked there would be a ringing around her, as if she was surrounded by an invisible halo of bells that shimmered when she spoke. There was something warm and frank about her that I liked right away, being neither warm nor particularly frank myself.

The first thing she said to me, shaking my hand and looking at the blue paint stains around my fingernails, was, *you're a painter.*

Maya and Jake befriended me. I would go to their apartment for dinner, and Maya would send me home with jars of soup and leftover lasagna. The rooms in the two apartments were identical in their layout. At first, being in their apartment was like visiting myself, except some stranger had removed and replaced all my belongings. Replaced my easel with two music stands, my cinderblock-and-board shelves with polished wooden bookcases, plunked down two loveseats where I had only open floorspace. Through the sliding doors I could see the same night view I saw from my balcony, but twelve feet higher. Light spilling from the opposite windows into the alley.

Maya and Jake moved around one another in the small apartment with easy domesticity, lightly touching one another's backs as they passed smoothly from refrigerator to counter to cabinet, or reached for the ceiling rack where pots and brassy pans reminded me of a healthy symphonic percussion section. Jake wore black T-shirts and an apron to cook, and the tattoo I'd first noticed in the museum was a crouched blue-black panther, inked with a highlight over its S-shaped backbone as it prepared to leap above its owner's elbow.

Maya and Jake together were how I imagined family life, although my own parents rarely cooked. When they were home from work at the same time, we would eat out, Thai food or Japanese. When my mother worked late or had meetings, my father would cook pancakes for dinner and heat syrup in the microwave.

Sometimes I would ask Maya and Jake to play for me. Their eyes sparked in the same way when they played together, she with her cello snug in the folds of her skirt, he with the fine, smooth violin tucked beneath his chin. The instruments emphasized the difference in their sizes; Maya grew smaller and more birdlike behind her cello, her thin arms light and strong as hollow bones. And Jake's hands were even larger around the polished wood neck of his violin. As he played, the great cat on Jake's forearm seemed to be creeping stealthily forward. Hunting, I thought. Or maybe just enchanted, a hapless cobra by a charmer's flute.

Watching them play was like watching a strange mating ritual. They looked up from the music at the same moments, breathed together at the beginning of a phrase. And in my sincere clapping afterwards, I realized that not only is painting an art without applause, it is also an art in which the artist is absolutely, necessarily, alone.

Omar is Jake's cousin. The first thing he said was, *It's going to snow*, as he hung his heavy coat in the closet, the day he carried the smell of cold into Jake and Maya's apartment. Omar had a slighter build than Jake, and darker skin and eyes. Protruding from a pressed white shirt, his wrists were fine and dark.

When I meet extraordinarily beautiful people, I always wonder if they know how beautiful they are. If their lives are more than ordinary, if strangers stop them in the streets to tell them they are stunning. If they know that wherever they walk they leave trails of lust pangs and broken hearts, like a cat leaving wet footprints. Omar carried himself with a cool pride that made me suspect that he knew exactly how handsome he was.

We were sitting in their living room waiting for water to boil, on couch cushions that sank down so far, I wasn't sure I'd be able to get out. They kept their curtains open even though the sun had set nearly three hours earlier. Outside, the bare knotted branches of cottonwoods were illuminated by the single streetlight on the back alley. Twigs like finger bones waved gently in a slight night breeze.

"Ivy's a painter," Maya announced to Omar.

He shook my hand, and his fingers were cold from the walk over, his nails scrubbed clean.

"What do you paint?" Omar wanted to know. I searched his face for some flaw, something to make him less than beautiful. Perhaps his nose was slightly crooked.

"Portraits," I said. "Figures."

"Of course," Omar nodded approvingly. "The body is beautiful." He turned his head slightly, and I saw I was wrong, his nose was lovely and symmetrical.

"Show your work to Omar," Maya said. "You could hang some of it at Mazatlan."

"My café," Omar explained. He reached for a wine glass with an elegant hand, fingers like leggy plains creatures.

The truth was, I only had four canvases to show anyone. The four paintings I'd kept were a series based on nudes and elm trees. It was the unreadable gesture of trees that had interested me, branches lifting up like arms, sometimes plaintive, sometimes victorious. Mourning women throw their arms up in lament, conquering warmongers in celebration. The rest of my art school work I'd left in a supermarket dumpster on the outskirts of Chicago. I'd dropped the lid with a metallic bang on two drifting flies, the smell of rotting. It had been an act of cleansing, of starting over. I'd felt light driving west.

But Jake and Maya and Omar were all looking at me expectantly, so I said, "Sure."

"Go now," Maya said. "We'll do the pasta."

So I led Omar downstairs to my apartment, which was nearly bare compared to Maya and Jake's. The main room had only my paints and easel and the dust balls that reappeared daily, magically condensing from empty air. The painting on my easel was a Georgia O'Keeffe exercise I'd been working on.

Omar stood contemplating the canvas while I retrieved my work from the closet.

"*Jack-in-the-Pulpit*," Omar named the painting. "It's the fourth of the series, painted in 1930. Oil on canvas."

"Impressive," I said admiringly, referring to his familiarity with the piece.

"Impressive," he echoed, turning his appraising eye from the painting to me.

I leaned my four paintings against the wall, and he considered them individually, arms clasped behind his back. His eyes were a dark shadow across his face. It was so quiet, I could hear Russell flipping in his bowl in the other room.

"This one is a self-portrait," he said, rather than asked.

"No," I said. "It's not."

Omar had the kind of deep-set eyes that always have a crescent shadow beneath them. It gave him a look of vulnerability and suffering. Those shadows made women want to mother him. Even though I've never had much of a maternal instinct, I found myself wanting to smooth his eyebrows, lick my finger and wipe the dried sleep from the inner corner of his eyes.

He looked at me finally and said, "You paint people as if you love them."

"I'd like to paint you," I said, honestly.

"These would look good in the café," Omar said. "Come by sometime, and we'll see where we can hang them." He glanced again at the O'Keeffe exercise, and we walked together back upstairs.

22

4

The first of Georgia's work that Steiglitz ever showed were the drawings she made kneeling on the floor of her bedroom when she was twenty-seven-years old. The drawings she made when she said she was tired of painting how she had been taught, and wanted to draw the shapes she had in her own mind. She drew on her hands and knees, cheap student sketch paper spread beneath her. Charcoal dust covered her palms and the knees of her dress.

Steiglitz saw those drawings and said, *Finally, a woman on paper*. And he hung them on the walls of his gallery, where Picasso's and Matisse's work had hung.

I want to explain what it is to paint on the best days. On the best days, it is a complete dissolution of yourself. But these are only words—how can I explain?

When I was fifteen, and first drawing, one of my assignments was to draw a bell pepper. I bought one at the market, an ordinary pepper with tight shiny skin and only a faintly spicy smell. I sliced a lobe off with a sharp knife, and suddenly, for the first time in my life, I really saw it. The inside of a pepper is a vaulted chamber. Water in the walls. Fine flat seeds. It was the most complicated thing I'd ever seen. As I drew, I forgot everything else.

On the best days, it is a concentration that is close to holy.

I think I have always expected love to be like this, and have always been disappointed.

5

I saw Omar the very next day after first meeting him. I was walking home from work the long way, by dirt paths in the foothills. The low afternoon sun cast long shadows everywhere. I walked along the frozen footprints in the dirt with my jacket zipped up to my nose. The skin on my hands was tight from the cold air, and I had them jammed in my pockets.

Omar must have seen me coming, but he didn't turn around. I was looking at the ground and didn't see him until I saw his shadow. A camera hung on a thin black strap around his neck. He was looking through binoculars at a speck over on the next hill.

"Look," he said, without a greeting, and handed me the binoculars. He stood very close behind me and pointed over my shoulder. My upper lip was damp from breathing in my coat.

"Cassin's Kingbird," Omar said. "You hardly ever see them this time of year. He must have lost his way."

Through the binoculars, I watched the bird preen and puff his feathers out, unaware of how lost he was.

Omar stood so close that I could feel his body heat through two thick jackets, and when he moved the lens of his camera brushed against my back. If I'd turned, my nose would have hit his chin. He took the binoculars back and watched until the bird flew away. Then he took a small dog-eared book from his chest pocket, and opened it to a page full of illustrations of red-bellied birds. He made a small note in pencil by one of the pictures.

"So I can remember when I saw it," he explained. I took the book from him and saw that on nearly every page, in meticulous handwriting, was the date and location of the birds he'd seen. "These are just notes," he told me. "I have a more detailed journal at home."

He tucked the binoculars in an inside pocket and held the camera to his eye, adjusting the lens settings with a series of deft movements. The afternoon was very quiet and the sound of the shutter was a sharp click.

It was starting to get colder, and the half of my face in the sun was warmer than the half in the shade. Omar looked older in the sunlight than he had in the night. I could see the beginnings of strain in the line between his eyebrows. His eyes were so dark I could hardly see where the pupil ended and the iris began. I was sketching him in my head. In the afternoon light, a dark drop-shaped shadow hung beneath his earlobe, and cheekbone to jaw formed an oblong plane.

"You're not working today?" I asked.

Omar glanced at his watch. It looked expensive, with smaller circular faces embedded in the main blue watch face. "I'm going back to close for the evening," he said. "Let me walk you home first."

I fell into step beside him. The evening air smelled of piñon and juniper bushes and the impending snow.

"I was serious about hanging your work at the café," he said as we walked. "We're going to rotate some photographs out next month, and we'll have wall space for you."

"I wish I had new paintings for you," I said. Part of me was surprised at how willing Omar was to show my work. Perhaps he thought of it as a favor for his cousin's friend. All the shows I'd been in before had been arranged through the art school, and my paintings had hung as one young voice amongst many, all clamoring to speak the same truths in a new way.

I told Omar that I'd been stuck lately, unable to paint anything I liked.

"Creativity comes in waves," he assured me. "Every artist I've known has had dry spells. Jake is like that, too. He's afraid that if he doesn't play the violin for a week, then he'll never play again. And he always does."

Omar's voice was warm. If you could see it, it would be an amber-colored voice, thick like honey.

"What about the O'Keeffe painting I saw at your apartment?" he asked. "That's something."

"It's just an exercise," I said.

Closer to the plaza, grey, leafless cottonwoods loomed in the streetlights. It was the time of day when the sky is still dove-grey, but all the streetlights and headlights clicking on make the dark come faster.

When we reached my apartment, Omar held my hand for a moment in both of his. His palms were very smooth and his skin cool.

"I'll see you soon?" he asked. I said that he would.

6

After meeting Maya and Jake, it was hard for me to remember Santa Fe without them. They became integrated into my life as naturally as two vines growing together. I saw Jake at the museum, of course. We would sometimes take breaks together and walk to buy soda or pretzels. Even in the winter, the sun was strong at midday and sometimes we would stand out back in the heat radiating from the wall. He seemed more talkative without Maya, or maybe he just talked more because I'm quiet. I asked him about the northern part of the state, where he'd grown up, and his family still owned ranch land.

"I think I've always been more attached to the land than Omar," he told me. "We spent summers there with our grand-parents as kids, even after he and his mom moved to the city." He always looked a little wistful when he talked about the ranch, and he would look away from me across the dirt-packed lot. "I don't get back much anymore," he told me. He and Maya both played in the orchestra for the Santa Fe Opera, and would have rehearsals nearly every day in the summer.

Jake played in a band, too, with a group of skinny, short-haired men who billed themselves as an Irish punk band, though only the lead singer had the fair freckled skin that I associate with the Irish. Maya, Omar, and I would go to their shows at Mazatlan or some other bar in the city. Seeing Maya in the younger, rowdy crowds, I was struck by how she seemed comfortable everywhere, how the authoritative English as a second language teacher in long skirts could part her hair at an angle, don jeans and heavy boots, and blend in easily. We would usually get to the shows early and find a table at the back, away from the tightest throng. I remember watching the band set up one night before a show, unwinding thick black cords and adjusting microphone stands. Jake stood alone on one corner of the stage, warming up with his microphone turned off. He pulled the bow in grand arcs over the strings. Maya rattled the ice in what was already her second drink of the night.

"There's something painful about watching someone you know on stage," she said. She didn't seem to be talking directly to Omar or me, she was just making an observation. "Knowing everyone in the room is watching the same person. Sharing them with the world."

Jake looked up as if he knew we were talking about him. He kept playing as he gazed in our direction, a smile toying with the corners of his mouth. I couldn't tell if he was looking at Maya or at me. I wanted it to be me, I realized. The violin looked tiny above his barrel-chested torso.

Maya put her hand on Omar's arm, and looked at him with the earnestness of one creeping closer to drunkenness. "When is he going to grow up, Omar?" she asked, seriously. "Do you think he will?"

Omar wore the same unreadable calm expression, as always. He didn't acknowledge her hand on his arm, but didn't shake it off, either. "You don't want him to grow up," he told her.

Maya laughed then, and her laughter filled the room, reached to the corners of the stage. Maya was always laughing. She laughed like bells.

"No, I guess I don't," she said.

When the lights dimmed and the drummer launched into his driving rhythm, I could feel Omar watching me watch Maya and Jake.

Maya and Jake came to sit for me once or twice a week that winter.

"I can't pay you," I told them, but they didn't mind. Sometimes they came together, sometimes just Maya came. Jake never came by himself. There are painters and there are models, and Maya and Jake were models. Meaning that they became more beautiful when everyone in the room was looking at them. They withstood, unflinching, the scrutiny of strangers. They shone.

I've had non-professional models before who were uncomfortable posing nude, but Maya and Jake were as natural and matter-of-fact without clothes as fully dressed. They would both sit with admirable stillness as I squinted my eyes, held my pencil at arm's length, measured relative lengths of torsos and limbs. Maya had a long, narrow waist and a womanly flare of hips. When she sat with her back to me she was the shape of a violin, the way women are supposed to be. Jake was thick-shouldered with a trickle of black hair running below his belly button.

They practiced talking without moving. When we ran out of things to talk about, we'd play the favorite game, which would go something like this:

Jake: What's your favorite ice cream?
Maya: Pistachio.
Me: Mint chocolate chip.
Jake: Chocolate fudge brownie.
Maya: Favorite color.
Jake: Blue.
Maya: Green.
Jake: What's yours?
Me: I don't have one.
Jake: You have to.
Me: No, I really don't.
Jake: Just pick one.
Me: Red.
Maya: Fruit.
Jake: Watermelon.
Me: Banana.

29

Maya: You guys are boring. Pomegranate.

Jake: That's not a fruit.

Maya: Of course it is.

Jake: Favorite body part for a tattoo.

Maya: Man or woman?

Jake: Both.

Me: You're moving. Go back to where you just were.

Maya: Back.

Jake: Ankle.

Me: Forearm.

Jake: What if it's a hairy back?

Maya: That's okay. I like hairy backs, too.

Jake: That's why you like me.

Me: Stop moving!

Jake: You pick a favorite.

Me: Favorite composer.

Jake: No, that's too intellectual. You're making my head hurt.

Maya: Puccini.

Me: Rachmaninoff.

Jake: Rage Against the Machine.

Maya: That doesn't count.

Jake: Yes, it does.

Maya: No, it's a band, not a composer.

Jake: Okay, the songwriter for Rage. What's his name.

Me: Do you guys need to take a break?

Jake: I could use a snack.

Whenever Maya and Jake were coming over, I would take my O'Keeffe studies into the other room and close the door. They weren't a secret, exactly; I can't explain why I didn't want them to see the paintings. They felt private. Perhaps each copy was an expression of my frustration with my own work. Or something private between Georgia and myself.

Maya saw those copies once. She'd wanted to see my old paintings, the ones that Omar was going to hang, and had followed me into the room where the O'Keeffe canvases leaned face against the wall.

"What about those?" she asked.

"They're nothing," I said, but she reached out and flipped the painting around. I felt strangely naked with Maya looking at the flower.

"O'Keeffe," she said. She looked at me for a moment with an expression I couldn't read, but then she just smiled and said, "It's good," and leaned it back against the wall.

On the days that Maya came alone, she would talk about growing up in Boston, in the small apartment above the small restaurant her parents owned. "A special occasion restaurant," she called it, with only four small tables and triple-digit wine. People would make reservations three weeks in advance, and come for anniversaries and engagements in tuxedos and once-a-year pearls. In the dark mornings, the sound of the garbage truck grumbled beneath her window, hauling away the rank restaurant waste, wilted spinach and half-eaten cheese.

Maya often stayed to eat after drawing sessions, and was always running upstairs for the right ingredient. My apartment was gradually transformed by her, my empty shelves lined with legions of cardamom, coriander, ground ginger. She brought me clippings from their houseplants. A sprouting avocado pit, suspended in a glass of water above my sink.

"You're going to be the greatest mom," I said one day when she'd come alone. For awhile we were quiet as I sketched, and there was only the noise of the charcoal scratching paper and crows calling outside my window.

"If Jake's ever ready," she said finally, and I saw the clumsiness of my comment and didn't know what to say. I looked back at the sketch pad, at the shadow I'd made near her eyes. It was too dark and I tried to blot it away with my eraser.

7

This is how it is to paint. First, you are struck by something. It can be a face, a tree, a vegetable, a stretch of road or an idea. Something about this road, face, or idea grabs hold of you and you know you must paint it; if not then, file it away someplace inside of you to come back to. Every painter has a stash inside of these faces, colors, and trees that they will paint one day. Then you sketch it, and start painting, and this is the point at which it really consumes you. You go to sleep at night thinking about it, planning the colors you'll mix the next day. This is the part I love, this is the moment when you are brilliant, your work is new and insightful—heart rending. This may last days or months, and will be punctuated by periods of doubt, when you think it is all wrong, everything is bad, insincere. But you come around, find new shades, and love it again.

Then when you finish the painting, there is a period of glowing adoration for what you've done. You think, this is exactly what I meant to say, the ultimate expression of my vision, the pinnacle. But one day, inexplicably, you'll see the painting from a different angle, or in different lighting, and suddenly it is a trite and talentless painting. You see how overdone the colors are, how haphazard and imprecise the lines, and suddenly you can't bear to look at it.

At first, I found this transition disheartening—it shakes your understanding of what is good, and right. How can something be pure and beautiful and true one day, and a cliché the next? It's a mystery like people falling out of love.

But I grew accustomed to it, and when I began to hate a painting I'd done, I would just throw it out or give it away.

But recently, I wasn't even starting anything new. I began to worry more and more about the fact that I wasn't really painting anything of my own. I had moved to Santa Fe to be a painter, I had constructed my entire identity around painting, and now that I couldn't produce anything that I liked, I felt as though I would evaporate into the desert air. In charcoal, I'd sketched pages and pages of figures, standing, sitting, reclining, but nothing in paint. I tried to do a self-portrait, but couldn't get past the ruthless charcoal sketch. If Bunny was right, and painting just means seeing, then I suffered from a debilitating inability to see myself. Perhaps this was just a different manifestation of self-love, that when I stood naked in front of a mirror I was alarmed at my complexity. Unable to render my hands, struck by the wrinkles on each knuckle. How could I sketch a belly with five thousand fine hairs?

Then, not painting began to color every moment of my day. It was distressing—like the inarticulate din of a neighbor's television tugging at the back of your mind, or like a slight tear in your contact lens always marring your vision. Somehow I'd lost my bearings. Working at the museum every day, I saw paintings so good that I wondered why I bothered. Georgia had paintings of bones that made me want to weep.

Just to feel a brush moving paint, I stretched and primed canvases with layers of white paint. I found myself turning more and more often to the O'Keeffe work. I copied from enormous posters I brought back from the museum, and from the memories of actual paintings that I studied during the day. The work was mechanical and soothing. I would calculate exactly the placement of the horizon and measure precisely one line against another. I finished my practice imitation of *Jack in the Pulpit IV*, and moved on to *Jack in the Pulpit V*, with a fingernail sliver of red sliced down the center; and then *VI*, which was really just a black-tongued stamen in an oblong tunnel of white. I liked the symmetry of her work, the way her paintings were almost split down the middle, but then leaned gently to one side.

Now I wonder what it means to paint another person's work.

For me, at the very beginning in art school, it was just to inhabit another pair of eyes. When people find out that you are an only child, they always ask, *weren't you lonely? Who did you play with?* And I try to explain the teeming imagination that every only child harbors, by necessity. The multiplicity of lives. I was never alone growing up, but surrounded by candy-striped acrobats and ferocious loyal pirates. From my room to our tiny urban backyard, I crossed circus rings and spuming seas. Perhaps trying to be Georgia was just the adult version of a desperate imagination. We all want to forget ourselves sometimes.

If I'd known what was going to happen, would I have done everything the same? I ask myself this and can't answer.

8

As I spent more time with Omar, I saw that he was prone to moody, quiet spells. Small things would thrust him into a melancholy silence, especially at the café. A rude customer would leave him simmering with his eyebrows drawn, and the muscles at his temples tight from a clenched jaw. He never said so, but I think what he wanted was respect. This may have been what drew us together, that he respected the paintings and drawings I'd done, and that I respected his quiet dignity.

We were walking one evening in the odd yellow light that follows a sunset in July. We walked through a neighborhood around the plaza, where the houses were mostly single-story with chain-linked backyards, and front yards that were in various stages of drought-induced sickness. An occasional dog barked, and the dog-owner shouted at him to be quiet.

"This terrifies me," said Omar.

"What?"

"All this. The houses, the yards, the TVs inside. The complacency. The dog that needs to be fed twice a day."

I knew what he meant.

Lights were on in every house, and through the windows the eyes of televisions blinked, slowly, furiously. Every house with a car and a television, the staples of security, of success, of being-a-member of society. The neighborhood spoke of weekends spent doing yard work, cutting grass, hauling branches, digging dandelions with three-pronged weeding forks, then back to work Monday.

I knew what Omar meant because I too feared that complacency, even as I envied it. I too wanted a house and a yard and a dog to love me, unconditionally. Sometimes I would imagine, *this is my house, here, that I'm coming home to. This is my car in the driveway,* and even in that pretending could feel how it was suffocating, how the world suddenly shrank, and opportunities dwindled. It was the becoming absolutely average, the nothing-to-look-forward-to but the births of nephews and nieces. It was the ultimate, final, decisive resignation of your dreams. When you buy a single-story home in the suburbs, and a backyard grill and a forty-pound bag of dog food, these decisions all say, *I am resigned. I have accepted that I will never be outrageously famous, I am not going to do anything to violently and radically shake the world, I will leave no profound and unmistakable footprint on our society.* It is to give up the freedom to hitchhike around the world with only a backpack, it is to acknowledge that you will never astonish great cities of men with your beauty.

And yet, secretly, we want this. We want a small house to call home, to decorate as we like, to have backyard barbecues with dogs and nephews and nieces. We want that life, envy it, crave it, and fear it absolutely.

"We'll never be like this," I told Omar, and he believed me.

We were at his apartment one day when business was slow at the café, and he'd left it in the charge of his server. Omar's apartment was darker than mine. His bare walls seemed defiant, as if to say that he was not going to live here long enough to bother to make a home. He'd been there for nearly four years, but it looked like he could pack up all his belongings and be ready to leave in a few hours.

His curtains were drawn, even in the day, which made his north-facing bedroom even darker. It was a bare room too, almost spartan, with a bed and a single lamp on a small table built of wood and concrete blocks. He had no book-case, but a stack of secondhand books on the floor. Dostoevsky and Marquez, Camus and Kundera. In another stack, several bird books with titles like *Feathers of North and South America*, and a Spanish-English dictionary.

From his bedroom, a sliding glass door led onto a small concrete balcony with a wire railing that was more decorative than practical. The railing gave the balcony a false sense of security, but with the slightest pressure I imagined that it would fold like cardboard, sending someone pitching three stories down, an unlucky rag doll.

Two mismatched socks waved stiffly from a folding clothes rack, the heel of one of the socks worn down to a few threads.

"You're brave," he said, leading me through his apartment to the balcony.

I thought he meant for standing on the balcony.

"No, for coming to a new city all alone."

He took a box of cigarettes from his shirt pocket and looked at me questioningly. He was not offering a cigarette, I noticed, but asking for permission.

"Not brave," I said. "Just curious."

The matchbook he used was from the café—MAZATLAN it said in bold red letters. The scrape and flare of the match were audible. After blowing it out, Omar placed the match with measured care on the thin railing. He exhaled carefully away from me.

"You know what they say about curiosity," he said.

The balcony was so narrow that even with our beat-up chairs pushed all the way back to the door, our knees nearly touched the railing. I stretched my legs, and let the toes of my shoes hang over the edge.

"I'm curious, too." Omar said.

"What are you curious about?" I asked.

He knocked ash over the edge and looked out across the dirt courtyard. "Oh, lots of things," he said. "Mexico City,

37

Katmandu, Bogota. The Andes. Migrations of swallows and lemmings."

I could see the beginnings of age in Omar in the afternoon light. Not through wrinkles or gray hairs, but the tensing of muscles around his eyes. I knew what he would look like as an old man, still thin, but the skin a little looser.

"I'm curious about girls who live alone and sleep on mattresses on the floor," he said.

Omar washed his hands before we made love that afternoon. He was self-conscious about the smell of his cigarettes. His lovemaking was like much else about him, serious and almost formal. Almost chivalrous. He watched my face the whole time, and held my head so I had to see him, too. He only closed his eyes once, at the end.

This is how these things always happen for me. There is no talking, there are no declarations of love; it is just two people who desire one another with nothing to discuss, and I tell myself this makes things simpler.

Afterwards, he sat smoking on his balcony, and I lay in his sheets. They smelled of detergent, which was reassuring, clean, but somehow impersonal. Omar always smelled of things. His citrus detergent, lavender soap, sometimes coffee, and occasionally cigarettes. But he had no smell that was only him, his body was the source of no aroma, his hair smelled of shampoo and his underarms of deodorant. Not like Jake, later, whose shampoo and deodorant smells were always mingled with the distinct animal smells of Jake's hair and Jake's saltiness.

I went and stood behind him in the open door, and smoothed his hair over his dark forehead. He lifted my hand from his head, kissed my knuckles and held my palm to his chest.

"I want you to know," he said, "you're the first girl I've been with in a long, long time."

He said this as though it were an offering, and I felt a small, inexplicable flickering of shame.

9

I loved Santa Fe and I hated Santa Fe, and that was not a contradiction. The things I love are often the same as the things I hate. That is not a contradiction; it is the difference between mornings and evenings. That is to say, no difference at all, except the tilting of the earth.

My paintings were on the walls at Mazatlan, and sometimes I went and sat there. Some people looked at them, but mostly they did not notice the walls, drank coffee and ate soups, talking of politics and love.

I liked to watch Omar work. His eyes were earnest when he spoke to customers. He washed the windows every day. I would sit inside and watch him through the glass. He never looked at me, but made big smooth soapy circles. I could see his shoulders swimming inside his shirt.

Sometimes when business was slow or he took a break, he would come sit with me or we would go together to the stoop out back. I would ask him about every bird I saw.

"Ash-throated flycatcher," he would say.

Sometimes he would recognize a birdsong and stop in the middle of a sentence, or hold up his finger to silence me if I was speaking.

"Western bluebird," he'd say, and I would listen through the city sounds for the call. Over time, I started noticing birds on my own, especially in the mornings and the evenings when they sang in droves.

Then, when he was off work, he would take my hand and we would walk together through the plaza, and the pigeons would all scatter when we walked by, like leaves falling up instead of down. At his apartment it was always very, very serious. He sometimes kissed me as though he were angry, or starving. Then he would apologize.

"I'm sorry. I'm sorry, do I scare you?"

"Can't scare me," I said.

It's funny how we love despite ourselves. We love instinctually, beyond the control of rationality, because we are programmed to love. Because, my mother might say, the survival of our species depends wholly upon the irrationality of love. And my father might counter that the propagation of ourselves was nothing more than the continuation of suffering. Of course, I didn't think about this with Omar, but I loved him and hated him, and that was not a contradiction.

There were times he was not serious, and if it was not too cold we would go outside and lie on our backs to look at the clouds, shape-shifting and formless.

"What do you see?" I ask.

"A big dragon," he says. "Breathing smoke. What do you see?"

"A bird. Now what do you see?"

"A dragon."

"But it changed."

"I see a different dragon now. What do you see?"

"An old man. That's his cane," I say.

"Now I see a boat," I say a little later.

"I see a dragon."

"What, still?"

"No, this one has a tail."

"I see Rhode Island."

"I see a dragon."

"Stop it."

"No, I really do. That's his wing."

"You have grass in your hair."

"You have grass in your hair."

"You have grass in your face."

40

"Now you have grass in your shirt."

"Stop!"

"You don't like grass?"

"It tickles."

"Are you crazy about me?"

"Yes."

"Say it."

"I'm crazy about you. Now you say it."

"You're crazy about me."

"Stop."

"Okay, I'm crazy about you."

Omar once told me that I look like Georgia, but he was lying. Her face is more defined than mine, her forehead higher, her nose stronger. In old group photos, you could pick Georgia out right away, not as a beauty, but as a self-sufficient presence. I look back at class photos from art school and if I didn't remember where I was seated, even I wouldn't pick myself out of the mass of young, idealistic faces. I am taller than Georgia was, I wear my hair parted in the middle. She wore black on black, simple shirts and dresses with white trim. I wear old jeans and bright thrift shop tees, except to work at the museum, for which I bought three identical V-necks, in hunter green, maroon, and off-white. I don't own anything black.

I've seen the early Steiglitz nudes of Georgia, and she is feminine in ways that I am not. Her waist tapers, she has strong thighs, and breasts made for feeding the children she didn't have. My legs are twiggier, my hips smaller in proportion to my ribs. When I gain weight it is in my belly, like a man. My cheeks are softer, my lower jaw more recessed. I have freckles. My front left tooth is crooked, but I don't know about Georgia, since she never smiles in her pictures. One thing that is similar, though, is our eyes. They sit back deep in our faces, so there are always shadows. Omar's eyes are like this, too, but he has double shadows, since the skin beneath his eyes is tinted a faint blue. I told him this once, and he said that hawks have eyes like this, deep and close together. *Predators' eyes*, he said, as opposed to the eyes of mice and rabbits, far apart, to see more angles. Anyway, Georgia and I, and I supposed Omar, see the world from a place deeper in our heads. Maybe the light that the world radiates changes slightly in the extra millimeter it has to travel to meet our pupils.

10

It was a dry winter. Snow came infrequently and did not stay long. January and February passed, and five days each week I would pull an overcoat around my shoulders, shove my hands in thin, ragged gloves into my pockets, and walk the fifteen minutes to the museum. I walked even on the coldest days, that left me at the gift shop with red cheeks and a running nose. I look back on this as a happy time in my life; still, some days I resented the work and something about it struck me as cruel. Not my particular work, but all work, cruel and suffocating. It was a happy time, but still I was not satisfied. Cruel of the world, I thought, to foster so much love. Cruel of the world to encourage curiosity and wonder and desire in children, when as adults we spend days locked in single-windowed rooms where passionless men and women pass through, trickling away their lives. Sometimes in the museum, the mediocrity of my life would seize me by the throat. In a panic, I searched the faces of the customers from behind the counter, not as an artist looks at faces, but as a man lost in a foreign country searches faces for one that may speak his language. I looked past bulbous noses and pinched nostrils and thick upper lips and sagging jowls and map-line wrinkles, searching for a slump of shoulder or a curve of eyebrow that might show me that they, too, wanted more. This is the panic I took home with me in the evenings: this can't be my life. That person, who worked seven hours at a time opening and closing the money drawer surrounded by scarved and perfumed women, I couldn't let that be who I was.

I poured myself wholly into the O'Keeffe exercises. Painting something, you take possession of it, claim it and know it as nobody else does. I am usually greedy in my painting, the way lovers gorge. But in doing the copies, my hunger disappeared. Instead of insatiable, selfish desire, I painted with focus, my brushes steady. And I did not feel alone, doing the imitations, but imagined that some essence of Georgia was in the room with me, my silent mentor.

Maya came over one day as I was sitting at my easel with a sketchbook. A recently completed O'Keeffe painting rested against my wall, drying. I hadn't been expecting her, but invited her in. She sat on the floor against my wall, her knees pulled up to her chest. I flipped to a new page in my sketchbook and drew absentmindedly while she talked.

"Do you believe in destiny?" she asked.

"No," I said.

"Coincidence?"

"I believe we look for coincidences and find them," I said.

Maya walked to my kitchen. The faucet roared on and a cabinet opened. I could hear by the rising pitch of the water as a jar was filled, and then heard her swallow. My charcoal scratched on the paper. She came and sat back down.

"Sorry, did you want water?" she asked.

"No, thanks." Funny, I didn't mind her being there. It seemed natural.

"Your O'Keeffe paintings," she said. "They're very good."

"Thanks."

"Extremely accurate."

"Thanks." I was beginning to feel embarrassed.

"You know you're talented, don't you?"

"Well," I said.

"You don't have to be modest with me," she said. "In fact, let's not be modest at all. You know you're brilliant. I know it. It's obvious looking at this that you're not an ordinary painter. You have a gift."

These are words that every artist wants to hear, of course, but they made me slightly uncomfortable. Her praise was too much, was extreme, it filled the room and jostled around.

"The coincidence," she said, as if to herself, "is that you moved downstairs from me."

I didn't see why it was such a coincidence.

"You're my destiny," she said. "Don't you see? I'm your destiny."

"What are you *talking* about?"

"I have something to tell you."

"Okay."

"It's a secret."

"Okay."

"A secret secret."

I put down my charcoal. "A secret secret," I said.

"Do you want to know what I do?"

"You teach ESL," I said.

"I also deal art," she said.

"Why is that a secret?"

"I have a buyer interested in your work," she said.

"But I haven't done any work," I said.

"Your work as O'Keeffe," she said, and then I began to understand. Not suddenly, but gradually. Sunrise gradually, tide-coming-in gradually.

"Of course, he doesn't know your name," she said.

Outside, birds and distant traffic.

"You mean sell them as originals," I said.

"This might be your destiny," she said.

It was one of those unexpected decisive moments in your life that you don't see coming, and hardly recognize when it's there; but in retrospect it stands out like a huge jutting cliff, where your life changed course. Where everything after is different from everything before. *How did I miss that?* we ask ourselves in disbelief, looking back over permanently altered lives. But instead of recognizing the moment for what it was, I just sat calmly on my stool watching Maya drink water

45

from a Mason jar, thinking I should buy some real drinking glasses—not to mention a drying rack—instead of leaving all my dishes out on towels to dry. I listened with one ear as she said she would take my paintings with her to New York . . . art specialist, she said, verification papers, she said. Private buyer. I heard these words, and outside a large black bird settled on the adobe wall and gave a throaty, protesting call. The difference between ravens and crows, according to Omar: ravens are larger, they fly alone. Crows are smaller, travel in groups, as in *a murder of crows*. Murder being the word for the group of them.

"Who would believe it?" I asked. "Everything I've copied is in the museum. Everyone *knows* they're in the museum. Who would buy that?"

"First of all, a quarter of the stuff in museums is fake," Maya said. "Who knows where the originals are? And the kinds of people who are buying these paintings don't give a damn if they're stolen. You don't have to do exact copies. Do something in the style of O'Keeffe. The recently discovered Pelvis Series number six. An early O'Keeffe study of the Grey Hills."

She stood up and took the jar back into the kitchen. When she reemerged, she stood leaning against the doorframe.

"You look kind of shocked," she said.

"No," I said. "I'm not. Really."

"Think about it," Maya said. "Just tell me you'll think about it."

She held my gaze until I felt uncomfortable and had to look away.

"You could be great," she said.

I turned back to the newsprint I'd been working on. The figure was awkward, with disproportionately long legs folded under a bird body. I reached to flip the page over, and my fingers left a sooty smudge on the paper.

"Okay," I said. "I'll think about it."

46

11

Don't think that any hesitation was out of questioning the morality of the thing. It was not stealing in any real sense of the word. I've never understood the importance attached to a name. If two paintings look identical, why would the name of the painter make one more valuable? It's petty celebrity worship, the desire to own something created by a famous person. It ceases to be about the art and instead is about a personality. Maybe I am an idealist, but I think art should transcend this. It should be about the painting, not the painter.

So why the hesitation?

12

The next day was my day off, and instead of drawing in my apartment, I decided to drive and think. I'd been meaning to go north, past Abiquiu, to the part of New Mexico Georgia had painted.

I took the road through Pojoaque, past all the casinos, parking lots already lined with pickups and old vans at ten in the morning. All the buildings clustered close to the road: gas stations, burnt-out diners, tourist shops selling kachina dolls and chile ristras. Like a two-dimensional stage set lining the highway, and behind the line of storefronts the desert started, hills spotted with blue-green junipers. In the distance, the carved red barrancas in the valley cast their knife-shadows into dust, and even further the Jemez Mountains loomed, rolling like a set of waves, charging the dusty shore.

When I broke past the towns, the land spread its wings and opened before me. The road was just a snaking scar winding between odd crimson hills, along the rocky and muddy Chama river. It was late spring, and I drove higher, gaining elevation. Light blue-white dustings of snow appeared in the shoulder blades of the hills.

Why didn't she sign her paintings? A few of the earlier ones, yes, but Georgia's later works are all unsigned, unclaimed flowers and landscapes. As if she didn't crave ownership, but was only reporting what she saw. As if a signature were selfish.

I'd been driving for nearly two hours when I saw a small, plain sign that said ECHO AMPHITHEATER. I turned left onto a narrow road that led towards the cliffs that had sprung up along the silent highway. There was an empty, ghostly parking lot and splintery rest-stop picnic tables. I stepped out of the car and was engulfed by silence. It took my ears a minute to adjust from the rush of tires on pavement.

An enormous rounded cave loomed six or seven stories high in the pinkish tan cliff. Formed, I read, by eons of carving wind and dripping water. A brown metal railing prevented tourists from climbing closer; and in the mouth of the gaping cave several boulders, car-sized, house-sized, had broken from the cliff and fallen, sometime in the past thousand years. The information sign directed me to look up and to my right, where at the apex of the cliff sat a rock formed by time into the shape of a lion. I looked and found it, a giant stony feline resting with his paws stretched out in front of him, king of the cave, ready to pounce down from his majestic height.

You could be great, Maya had said.

This was the country that Georgia painted.

One hundred years ago, a hapless, greedy cowboy had led his cattle astray over these mountains. Like a fairy tale sorcerer, the Indian summer fooled him into leading his stock too far, too high. When the curtain of snow dropped, the cowboy had to choose, and like a human does, he chose his own life. He struggled with his horse, a flickering dark spot in the blizzard, and arrived back at the camp with frost-eaten toes and a heart too close to dead for grieving. But after warm whiskey by the fire, perhaps he thought of his cattle mewing stupidly into the snowflakes. They stayed standing until they were dead, and their bones were stripped first by coyotes, then turkey buzzards, then year after year of drying seasons and freezing seasons. Until one summer when Georgia stopped walking and bent at the knees to examine the sun-licked spine of a steer. Vertebrae protruded like dry white sea anemones. She wore a broad hat in the sun, and perhaps clouds gathered, blue-grey around the mountains.

She picked up the snakey spine, brushing away caked dirt and ants.

Here are some things I want: I want a house in the desert with great sliding glass doors and a garden with carrots and basil. I want bright, drowning sunshine every day of the year, even when it is cold out, even in monsoon season, and the rains will last only an hour. I want everyone to know what I see and I want never to be misunderstood. I want to make people I've never met cry because they see I understand. I want people who have never met me to fall in love with me. I want everyone I know to love me, voraciously. As voraciously as I love Georgia.

My parents' friend Bunny once told me that the human condition is longing. I'm not sure why she chose sixteen-year-old me to talk with about the human condition, but I suspect she spoke that way with everyone. Her conversations were whimsical and directionless. She would talk about the human condition in one sentence and then the perfect recipe for clam chowder in the next. I would find myself sifting through our conversations in retrospect, picking out her extraordinary wisdom like sorting peas. At the time I didn't know what she meant when she talked about longing, and I'm still not sure, but it is something that everyone shares. Maybe it is just a trick of our genes; maybe that is what drives our awkward coupling and reproduction. With each new person we think *maybe you, maybe you are what I'm missing,* and maybe for a moment the longing is quenched.

I sometimes imagine God—I don't believe in Him. He was, for my parents, strictly an intellectual curiosity and I inherited their calm skepticism; but I sometimes imagine him creating the world and he says, *Here, pilgrim. Here, take this impossible world. Take the first leaves on the baobabs, take the smell of tomatoes, take the shadows and the wing beats of a flock of afternoon pigeons, take it.* God says, *Here, you in your baby skin, take the reflection of the sun on impassive cliffs, take the scream of ravens, take a world that cycles through four* seasons. *Take it all, with one condition.* God says, *Take longing too, and know that you will never be satisfied.*

This doesn't justify my decision, or even explain it. I just wanted to tell you.

It was dark by the time I returned to my apartment, and I found Omar waiting outside the building.

"What's wrong?" I asked, alarmed.

"Where were you?" he demanded.

"It was my day off. I went up past Abiquiu. What's wrong?"

He drew me towards him, softly. His cheek was smooth against my temple.

"I was *worried* about you," he said.

Later when his sighs deepened to the breathing of sleep, I lay with my back to him, my spine curled against his warmth, and wondered how long it had been since anyone worried about me, and couldn't remember.

13

I went to see Maya one evening when I knew Jake would be out practicing with his band. She made green tea and we sat in their boxy chairs. Like their couch, the cushions were the kind that are hard to climb out of, thick as quick-sand. Maya sat cross-legged, her stocking feet folded beneath her, holding the mug with both hands. I sat engulfed by the chair, leaning my head back.

"This wind," I said.

"It sounds different at night, doesn't it."

There was sheet music on the coffee table, dark with six-teenth notes and double stops. I looked at the run of notes and tried to imagine what it would sound like. The notes looked like trilling birds.

"I was thinking about our conversation the other day," I said.

Maya waited. Steam curled like smoke from her tea. She exhaled slightly and the steam dipped forward, a shape-shifting ghost.

"I'll give it a try."

Maya nodded. "Good," she said. "Good."

I felt a small shift in the landscape of our friendship, as if we were walking over dunes of dry sand, grains slipping with each step. Sinking, sliding, choosing our steps carefully.

"What should I . . . is there a painting you want me to do?"

"Is there something you want to do?" Maya wasn't taking the lead this time. I had to navigate my own desert; it was freeing and intimidating.

"Maybe one of the church paintings," I said. "That style."

She nodded. "I'm going to New York in May," she told me. She set her mug on the coffee table by the music. It was nearly full. A faint dusting of tea leaves had settled on the bottom, the tea clean and golden. "Do you think you could have something ready for me by then?"

I looked back at the sheet music. I could see where Maya had marked it in pencil. *Piano. Crescendo. Look up.* Some of the notes were hooked together with tiny V-shaped marks.

"Does Jake know?" I asked.

Maya picked up her lukewarm tea again, held the mug against her cheek.

"We don't tell each other *everything*, you know," she said.

Part II

"I have to get along with my divided self the best way I can."

—Georgia O'Keeffe

14

Georgia wore gloves while she painted. She stood, wrapped in a Navajo blanket in the cold. Her car twenty feet away, a Model A with high windows. There was no road, only two worn lines on the earth, pocked and lumpy with stones. Tufts of grey grass straggled up the middle, between ruts. It was 1933 and men around the globe took a deep breath between wars.

Georgia was neither a young woman nor an old woman. Her eyes were bright, and she wore her hair long, knotted at the nape of her neck. She carried enough meat for three days, and kept it below the car out of the sun. When night came, she would move it to the roof, away from animals. Between where she stood and the car a small cedar fire smoked in a steady trickle. She tended the fire all day to warm the ground where she would sleep. The wind was very far away, on the other side of the hills, and she could hear the movement of a wet paintbrush over canvas.

In the nights, coyotes sang like moonstruck birds.

15

The spring equinox came and went, and days and nights balanced, then tipped to the other side. It had been a dry winter, and there was a week, maybe two, of melting snow. Grass was green in optimistic patches, tentative purple flowers uncurled beside the trickling arroyos. Birds felt the spring. Chickadees braided twigs into labyrinthine nests, flycatchers snapped young grasshoppers. But there was barely enough water to whet your appetite; it evaporated and was sucked into the earth almost as quickly as it melted. The top of Santa Fe Baldy melted from white to green to a crisp dry gold. The New Mexico spring is different from spring in Boston, where the trees are gaudy with pink lace. Spring in the desert is angry with wind. Days start like quiet songbirds, but at midday become the throaty call of an oil-winged raven. Then the wind begins, rattles budding cottonwoods, pushes crocuses back underground.

None of the buildings around the plaza downtown stand more than two stories tall. They are mostly adobe with thick wooden tree-trunk beams. In this city built of mud and trees, the tallest building is the cathedral, a block past the east side of the plaza. I've seen light in the afternoon shine down the street and glow off the cathedral in a way that would make an atheist believe.

The bar where Jake and I would sometimes go after work had a narrow wooden deck overlooking the plaza. I drank dark cold beers, but he would only ask for soda because his father was an alcoholic and his grandfather was an alcoholic and his mother was prone to drink too much when she wasn't weaving. This is the kind of bridled control that Jake had, that of an alcoholic who chooses not to drink. The day that he'd stopped drinking he'd gotten a tattoo to remind himself, he told me. He'd been hit by a drunk driver while he was on his motorcycle, sober. He said the only thing he could tell me about the accident was the noise, metal on metal, metal on asphalt, the thick rasp of a body sliding against the road, all muted by a larger, sourceless scream, he said, as if the world itself were splitting. He spent three days in the hospital, and walked out with one deaf ear and a new-found respect for life.

"I met Maya a week later," he said.

"I didn't know you had a motorcycle," I said.

From the second story, we were eye-level with the branches. Tight cones of new leaves were just beginning to uncurl.

I said, "I've been thinking of getting one."

"Are you going somewhere?" Jake asked.

"Maybe," I said. "Maybe Mexico. Panama. Maybe I'll ride down to Tierra del Fuego."

"Really." Jake began drumming the balcony railing with his left hand, using all his fingers. Below us on the plaza, I watched the tops of peoples' heads and imagined them all in a giant game of chess. Green benches lined the intersecting walkways. On one bench a white-haired man sat with a cane leaning next to him. Pink bits of his head showed beneath his white combed hair.

I ordered another beer.

"Do you ever get restless living in the same place?" I asked Jake. "Where would you go if you could go anywhere?"

"I've lived here all my life," he said. "I'm happy here."

"But what if there's someplace you would be happier?" I asked.

"People who think like that are never happy."

I lifted my bottle, and a breeze lifted my napkin from the balcony railing where it was resting. It swirled away from

58

Jake and me, lifting up and then blowing sideways, drifting to the plaza. The napkin scuttled along the ground and stopped at the leg of the bench where the elderly man sat.

Jake began to speak again. "I guess I'd like to live on the ranch again. To be outside all day, working hard in the sun."

"What's holding you back?" I asked.

"I don't think Maya wants to go. She loves the city, her job is here."

The beer was very cold and bitter. My hands were cold from the condensation on the bottle. I put my hand on my neck and felt the cool dampness on my skin.

"I'm afraid of getting back into that lifestyle," Jake said after awhile. "There's a lot of drinking, tobacco. Maya keeps me clean." He took a breath, and shifted in his chair so his knee was touching mine.

"I met Maya auditioning for the orchestra, and she helped me get the job at the museum." Jake said. Our bones tapped through the light cotton of his pants. "It's strange how your life just forms itself without you thinking about it."

"Maya got you the job at the museum?" I said.

"She knows everyone," Jake said.

I drained the rest of my beer and set the bottle down on the wood, right on its own damp-circle footprint. Jake reached over and began peeling the paper label off the bottle.

The old man on the plaza slowly bent forward and retrieved the napkin. He rose using his cane, and walked purposefully, unhurried, to throw it away.

16

I envy those who are satisfied to only look.

I have always been greedy, and beautiful things fill me with an insatiable hunger. It is not enough to see the bold red desert cliffs, I want to carve my name in capital letters across their faces. I see sapphire mountain lakes and I want to crawl into them and drink them down. I wanted to reach into Georgia's paintings, to tear past canvas stretched over balsawood, to grasp the gaping sky and roll in the blanched bones. I wanted to possess them and to know them like nobody else had ever done.

Gluttony greed lust sloth wrath pride envy.

I do not believe in God, but I sometimes imagine Him judging. I do not believe but I imagine white robes, curled and shadowed like calla lilies. *Forgery's not on the list*, I say. *Envy*, says God. *Greed Lust Pride*, He says. He has a wooden gavel carved from an oak, one hundred centuries old. It falls like lightning striking a nearby tree and the world shudders.

17

From the road, you can only see the back of the Ranchos de Taos church, which is how Georgia painted it, many times. It is not a building with straight lines, flush lines, but the walls swell and curve outwards as if the church will burst. Before I saw the building, I thought it was only in Georgia's eyes that the building arched like imperfect pottery, but the real church is as bowed as her painting of it. I half expected to see the makers' fingerprints in the adobe walls.

Georgia said that every painter in New Mexico must paint this church, as every artist must paint a self-portrait. She stood behind this hand-formed church on a stormy day in 1930. From the clouds in the painting, I can see that it was July. Storm-blue clouds, the kind that stir wind and make ten thousand cottonwood leaves rattle.

It was windy in April, too, but there were no clouds that day. I'd brought a folding chair and sat with my sketchpad on my lap. I sat in the sun wearing sweaters, and the air was cold on my hands. When I made dark lines, the wind blew and dragged charcoal dust in fine streaks across the sketch.

It is not an ornate church. Two bell towers flank the front, and the small windows are not graced by stained glass. From above, the church is shaped like a cross, in anticipation of God looking down from a distant height. It took more than forty years to build the church. I do not believe in God, but am awed by the perseverance He inspires. The way people will work, self-effacingly, for something great.

The composition of her painting is simple. Only the ground and the sky and the church. There is no sign of human life. It is as if the building sprang up spontaneously from the desert and the ceiling beams lay down of their own accord. The adobe buttresses extend all the way to the sides of the canvas, as if to ensure a complete separation between heaven and earth. As I drew, I wondered if the church joins the two or divides them.

Churches are made of dirt as man is made from dust. Adobe hardens and withstands the rain, and the foundation of dirt and water survives season after season of monsoons. Why doesn't the city dissolve and send our homes running down the gutters in muddy torrents? Why don't we dissolve? Each cell is seventy percent water, with the nuclei and ribosomes floating around inside the thinnest of membranes. Yet we withstand the rain. Somehow we are held together like mud-straw dwellings. Imagine stepping out into the rain and dissolving, flesh melting from soul, heartaches and fears and joys quenched in the gutter with so many muddy homes.

Every drawing, like every written word, begins with a line. There are different kinds of lines: straight lines, curved lines, thick lines and thin. Dark, light, broken, jagged lines. Every line creates a new dichotomy. Suddenly, where there was one thing, there are two. It is a separation. One side of the line is defined in contrast to the other side. As when one cell pinches into two, or when birth makes two animals from one.

A line may be many things. In front of you, a line may be the horizon. One side dirt and the other air. You may walk all the way to this line, only to find another elusive line, equally promising, equally distant. If a line is below you, it may be a ridge or a tightrope. You must keep your balance, or fall to one or the other side, but never both. Some people have lines drawn around them as protective, immutable cages.

Sometimes a line may run right through you.

18

I showed Maya the sketches I'd made of the Ranchos de Taos church with the strange feeling that I was exposing myself. She pressed her lips together and pulled her thin eyebrows in. She leafed thoughtfully through the sketchbook. I'd done more than a dozen sketches of the church at different angles. Some sketches filled the whole page, in others I'd let more of the horizon show.

"These are drawings of the church," Maya said, unnecessarily.

"I wanted to get a feel for it before I started painting," I said.

Maya nodded. "Of course." Her hair was twisted up elaborately behind her and held in place with a ballpoint pen. She had probably pulled it back hurriedly, without thinking, but the effect was as intricate as if she'd spent her morning in front of the mirror. "But you're not making a painting of the church."

I'd thought that was exactly what I was doing.

"You're making a painting of a painting," Maya said. "It's not how Ivy Wilkes sees the church that matters, it's how O'Keeffe sees the church. Ivy Wilkes isn't part of the painting." She said this without seeming unkind, and I imagined it was the same voice she used to explain irregular verbs to her students.

She reached for the large handbag she had brought, with two brassy buckles, and handed me a large manila envelope. It was substantial in my hand and unsealed. I pulled out a glossy stack of eight by eleven photographs, all of paintings by Georgia.

They were not the standard postcard-like representations of artwork, but scientific photographs; pictures that rendered the paintings as specimens. Meticulous, academic, categorized dissections. Frameless, the paintings had been photographed from the front, back, and edges. It was like seeing a moth spread and pinned on velvet. On the upper right corner on the back of each photograph was a date, June 11. Evidently they were recent.

Most of the photographs were of two of Georgia's paintings of the Ranchos de Taos church, one with a clear, blue sky and distinct lines, and the other beneath a monsoon-grey storm cloud, where the church was grainier and less distinct from the landscape. The third painting captured by these photographs I recognized immediately. It was Georgia's 1945 pelvis painting, red and yellow. I recognized it because it was in the museum.

"Where did you get these?" I asked.

Maya didn't answer. Her eyes were steady and unreadable. She had changeable eyes, they flirted between green and grey.

I flipped back through the stiff sharp corners and looked more closely at the stormy Ranchos painting. It was also a painting that was in the Georgia O'Keeffe museum. I knew exactly where each of the two paintings hung, one in the far room on a wall by itself, and the other between a jimson weed and a grey hills landscape. I couldn't understand how Maya had gotten these photographs. It was alarming, like seeing a nude photograph of yourself that you don't remember being taken.

"Did you take these pictures?" I asked.

"Will they help you?" Maya asked in turn.

It's illogical, I know, the objection I had to the photographs, which had obviously been taken illegally. Illogical for one who is planning to break the law to oppose a law broken. I can rationalize my feelings by saying that the photographs seemed a violation of Georgia's work, while my illicit paintings would be homage. Or perhaps they frightened me because they suggested that there were more people involved—a skilled photographer with access to a private darkroom, not to mention someone with the ability to enter the museum without being detected by security cameras. It seemed to me that I was sinking in more quickly than I had intended, that the ground was looser than I had anticipated.

But the photographs would undoubtedly help, and I said as much to Maya.

It took me only ten days to make the first painting of the church. First I studied the photographs that Maya had given me, along with any other reprints I could find. I would stare at the paintings in the museum, trying to permanently imprint them on my mind. Looking closely, I could tell what size brush Georgia had used, and where she'd used a palette knife; I could tell which color she'd put down first, and if she had let it dry completely before adding the next layer.

Then I started sketching. I worked in charcoal to get shape and shadow. This eventually became second nature to me, but at first it forced me to see where Georgia used strong lines and where her shades were blended. I began to see how Georgia's eye liked to organize a canvas, how much she loved the sky, and her own sense of symmetry.

After a series of charcoal sketches, I started painting. I only had to use one canvas, because I knew my work well enough not to make mistakes. I used oils from Winsor & Newton, just like Georgia, that Maya had given me. Because I wasn't copying paintings, just working in her style, I didn't have to reproduce Georgia's colors exactly, but I tried to mix shades similar to ones she might have used. Before the first layer of paint, I sketched a very light outline of the basic shape using a light carbon pencil. I've always done this, though some painters don't. It is like building a scaffolding before the house. Then I lay down the first blocks of color with a thick brush, and over a few days added spare layers of paint to complete the canvas.

Maya had said that I didn't want to see the church, I wanted to see how Georgia saw. I wasn't painting a church but painting a painting. A painter transcribes a three-dimensional world to a two-dimensional canvas via the medium of her mind. I was transcribing from two dimensions to two dimensions, and I cut out any evidence of my own mind. A painter by definition includes part of herself in the work. But in my case, there was nothing of me on the canvas. It was an act of self-erasure. My job was to be invisible.

How can I explain how I felt, looking at that first completed painting? I saw it with the pride of a skilled craftsman; it was impeccable. I could have hung it on the smooth museum walls and it would not have been out of place. I stood back from the easel and a faint thrill ran through me. It was more than pride. It was a kind of awe, because I had conjured the dead.

But the longer I stood, the more the thrill dulled, and gave way to a kind of sadness. Because it was only paint on canvas. When you see a painting in a museum by Georgia, it is not only art but artifact. That is, history. You have the knowledge that it was Georgia's hand that held the brush laying that exact paint. Which of course was missing from this painting, but nobody would know it. Here is my sadness: how easy it had been. Or not easy, but how *possible* it had been, to recreate in all superficial ways Georgia's work. It took an element of mystery out of her paintings.

When I showed it to Maya, she eyed it for a few moments without saying anything. She stepped close and bit her bottom lip, then stepped to the side and considered it from an angle. A small crease in her cheek deepened, then she smiled. Maya had thin lips, but a full smile that revealed all her tiny teeth. Then she was laughing. She looked at me, and I suddenly felt elated.

She reached both her arms around me, and we both laughed, a giddy laughter that was almost innocent in its joy, like we were kids at a summer camp, plotting the best prank in the history of the world.

After the first, I made two more paintings of the church from slightly different angles and in slightly different shades. The first two were summer paintings, with vivid blue New Mexico skies. The third was stormier, and I carefully studied the photographs to see how Georgia had rendered the storm clouds. In her painting, the clouds had the same grainy texture as the building, and I made mine the same.

The plan was this: Maya would take my paintings of the church to New York, to show to her friend Eric, an art historian with conveniently flexible morals. I didn't know if that was his real name, and I didn't know his last name, but I imagined an athletic man with a Roman nose, silver hair, and a two-hundred-dollar haircut. If he approved of the painting and thought it could sell as an original, he would provide the documentation to give the painting a "history"—records of previous owners, gallery showings, etc. Then he would sell the work to one of his network of international clients, keep forty percent of the money, and Maya and I would split the rest.

I remember one teacher from my first year of art school, Muriel James. We were doing self-portraits, and she admonished us to paint ourselves not as we would like to be, but as we are. Not to invent shadows that make our jaws stronger or our cheeks thinner or our clavicles more defined. We all persist in harboring an idealized view of ourselves, physical or otherwise. Such as: in my ideal vision of myself, I paint only for myself. I paint only because I love to paint, and am satisfied with my own unlauded expressions of beauty. I need no approval or admiration from my parents or teachers or peers. This is all true, sometimes. But there is a part of me also that craves recognition, a thrill I get from praise. It is a luxury of those who are adored to be able to shun others' opinions, as it is a luxury of the overfed and affluent to decry gluttony and wealth.

19

One afternoon Jake stopped by the gift shop as I was counting the money for the day and asked if I wanted to go to Omar's café with him.

It was one of the warmest evenings of the spring and the wind had died down as the sun set.

We sat at a table on the patio and waited for Omar. The sky was just fading into night, and in the west there was still a lighter blue strip above the mountains. The north star was out already, and a steady red planet. There was a reaching cottonwood in the middle of the patio and some sticky, curled buds had dropped onto the table along with wisps of cotton. Jake picked up a small bud and rolled it between his fingers, and smelled it.

"My mom used to hate the cottonwoods in our yard," he told me. "They're so thirsty. The roots stretch out ten times the size of the tree. She said they sucked all the water from her other plants."

He lifted a piece of cotton and placed it in my hair.

"Thirsty trees," he said. "If you're ever lost in the desert, climb a hill and look for a row of cottonwoods. They'll lead you to water."

The patio was lit by three lights on the side of the café building. The one on the far right was flickering, about to die. All the kamikaze springtime night bugs were dive-bombing into the lights.

"Do you know the constellations?" he asked after a while.
"No. You?"

"No. Except there's the Big Dipper. And Cassiopeia. Pegasus."

"It seems arrogant," I said. "Looking for human shapes in the stars."

Then Maya was standing behind us.

She said, "I thought I saw you from the street."

She smiled at me. "You've got cotton in your hair, silly," she said, and picked it out. The metal legs of the chair scraped on the patio as she sat down. She reached back to her hair, which was twisted in an elaborate knot and pulled out a pin. Hair tumbled down to her shoulders, and she exhaled as if a great weight had been taken from her. She began to massage her head with two hands.

"I got my ticket today," she said, matter-of-factly.

I didn't trust myself to speak.

"To Boston?" Jake asked.

Maya nodded. "I'm going to visit family," she said to me; and even though I knew she was lying, I almost believed her.

Behind Maya, I could see a bump in the patio where the cottonwood roots tunneled, searching for water. The tiles were raised like a mole's burrow. An underground maze. I wondered how long it had taken for the roots to push that far.

I could hear the sizzle patter of wings on light bulbs.

Maya sat with her back to the light, and I could barely make out her features in the backlit halo of her hair. It was easy to sit across from her and watch her talk, and not think about her selling my paintings. She and Jake were talking about the opera music they had to rehearse. Then she was talking to me.

"You'll be seeing a lot less of this boy," she said.

"What?"

"I only work half time at the museum when opera rehearsals start," Jake explained.

The light on the far right gave one final burst, flickered, and extinguished itself.

Just then, Omar came out and pulled a chair between Jake and me. He looked happy and more relaxed than usual. His shirt glowed white in the night. The table was white metal, and there was a hole in the middle for an umbrella on a sunny day. The cottonwood leaves rattled above us and wisps of cotton floated down. Jake reached out and caught a piece.

On the street beside the patio a car drove by, then another. I watched the shadow of the cottonwood swing around from the headlights. After a car passed, I was blind for awhile, then my eyes readjusted. I could feel Maya looking at me. Jake and Omar were talking. Maya's hand was resting on her knee, and Jake reached over, put his hand over hers and slipped his fingers between hers.

I looked at Omar's profile, his sharp high cheekbones and his sharp shaved jaw; then they were all laughing at something I hadn't heard. I was suddenly very tired.

I said I thought I'd head home, and Omar took my hand for a moment as I was leaving. Maya waved with jingling bracelets, and Jake saluted.

The café was on a one-way street, and the sidewalk was narrow. There were not many people out, and I walked with my hands in my pockets. It smelled like spring, new leaves. I stopped on a small bridge over the arroyo. The bottom was not far down, maybe twenty feet. Usually it was dry, but there was a trickle of water from the snow melt in the mountains. I couldn't see it but I could hear it. My shadow fell into the shadows of the arroyo. It was choked with brush, shrub oak and Chinese elm. I wondered if Maya and Jake would get married.

A little way off I could see the outlines of skateboarders in the park. They were riding in the dark, wheels screaming on concrete. A group stood to the side, and I saw the quick flame of a lighter, then darkness. There were more stars now. I tried to find the red planet I'd seen before, but couldn't see it.

When I walked into my apartment, I didn't feel like turning the light on. In the dark, I tapped some food into Russell's bowl; and from the streetlights outside my window, I could see his dark body poke to the surface to eat. I didn't undress, but lay with my clothes on and a blanket over me. I lay awake for a long time. Maya and Jake came home and I heard them moving above me, then they were quiet and I didn't hear anything but my own ears faintly buzzing.

20

May began without rain. The grass turned from the brief, hopeful snowmelt green to a crisp brown, and then shrank to patches on the cracked dirt. Even the golf course and the cemetery lost their lush green. Lawns in the desert are not lawns, but patches of rocks or gravel decorated with carefully placed cacti. The dryness was relentless, and in the dry evenings even the crickets seemed to be asking for rain beneath a star-brilliant, cloudless sky.

The night before Maya was supposed to go to New York, I lay awake staring at my ceiling. I don't have to do this, I thought. I could refuse to let Maya take the paintings, it could all be innocent. We could laugh about it in a few years, *remember the time I almost . . . silly me*. Like walking barefoot to the edge of the cliff above a lake, peering down, maybe even curling your toes over the edge, then deciding to turn around. I could decide! My life would be easy again and guiltless. I would walk to the museum in the mornings and home in the afternoons, I would see Omar and learn about birds. I would paint Omar, I thought, innocent in blues and yellows. It's not too late, I thought. It's not too late.

I called Maya.

"Who's that?" I heard Jake ask sleepily.

"I'm coming downstairs," Maya said.

She sat beside me in my bed in the light of a single lamp. She brought me a glass of water. It was strange and motherly.

"I don't think this is a good idea anymore," I said.

"What are you afraid of?" she asked, not unkindly.

"It's against the law," I said. "We're lying."

"What's the law?" Maya asked.

"I don't know. False reproduction, false sale of artifact . . ."

"No, I mean what is the law for? What is the purpose of any law?"

I didn't know.

"Do you ever drive above the speed limit?" she asked.

"Sure."

"Laws are for the common good," she said. "To keep humans from hurting one another. There are good laws and there are utterly idiotic laws. It used to be illegal to be gay. But don't you see, Ivy, we're not causing any harm. We're inflicting no suffering."

Her eyes were wide and brown and clear, and she truly believed everything she said.

"We're bringing a piece of art into someone's life who otherwise wouldn't have had it."

"Are you scared?" I asked.

"Scared of what?"

"Being caught."

"I won't be caught."

"What if you are?"

"I'll lie."

"What would they do?"

She shrugged.

"Would we go to jail?"

"Nobody's going to jail."

"Would you tell who did the painting?"

"Of course not."

"What if they offered you a deal?"

"I swear that I will never tell anyone that you are the creator of these paintings, even if they offer me twenty million dollars and threaten to pull out all my toenails."

"Okay."

"Now you say it."

"What?"

"Promise you won't tell."

"I promise," I said.

I drove Maya to the airport for her trip to New York. My canvases were rolled in the trunk in an anonymous cardboard tube. She was taking the three church paintings I'd done and a few of the earlier studies to show the dealer. Driving, I was aware of the paintings in the back as one is aware of a lover across a crowded room.

The road from Santa Fe to Albuquerque is broad and empty beneath a broad and empty sky. There is none of the drama of the northern part of the state, the screaming red hills and sudden mesas. There are few landmarks and few colors, the earth is thirsty in shades of tan and brown. Reservation land is separated from interstate land by a flimsy wire fence, strung on crooked metal posts. Close to the cities there are telephone lines, and their thin curves swoop and cut the sky. But in the middle of the drive the wires disappear, the billboards disappear, you can see a single cloud eighty miles away. The spots of cloud shadows are clear and harmless on the desert floor.

I drove with the windows down and a great roar of dry air filled the car. Maya was in high spirits. Her hair lifted from her shoulders and blew in her face as she leaned forward. I had my left arm out the window and was riding waves of air with my hand, letting the wind push me back, and then falling forward. We flew down the hill that descends from the Santa Fe plateau. We were still forty miles from Albuquerque. The day was clear, the sky a startling blue.

"Look," Maya pointed to a red spot in the distance, near the horizon. "A hot air balloon."

She looked over to see if I could hear her. "You don't usually see them this time of year," she said.

I wondered if the balloonist could see us. Flustered rushing ants.

Maya put her window down all the way and the air hit me harder from that side. My hair streaked into my eyes. In the distance, the Sandia Mountains loomed, blue on a blue sky.

By definition, a forgery earns that name only when it is represented as an original. There was nothing false about any of my paintings. The canvas was real canvas, stretched on a real frame; the paints were true paints, spread with a true brush. A signature would have been false, but Georgia didn't sign her work. The pastiches I'd made before meeting Maya were not forgeries but exercises. Once sold, the nature of the paintings would change entirely because the intention behind them had changed. So what makes a thing false?

Honesty is an abstract and capricious concept. The woman who knowingly sleeps with a married man is worse than the woman who sleeps with the married man who wears no ring. Ignorance is not only bliss, it is innocence.

"How fast are you going?" Maya shouted.

"Seventy."

"Speed limit's seventy-five."

I let my foot down a little harder on the gas. With a single practiced gesture, Maya pulled herself out of her seat until she was sitting on the window frame, her body outside the car and her heavy boots on the seat. Her left arm was in the car, her thin ringed fingers gripping the handle above the passenger window. Her shirt flapped, raging around her thin frame. She yelled a single joyful whoop.

A semi truck bellowed towards us from the south, and passed us with a slam of air and a sharp roar. In the rearview mirror, I saw a pair of sunglasses pitching along the dashed line in the middle of the road. They bounced twice, tiny and shining in the big land, and disappeared beneath the wheels of the truck.

Maya let herself back into the car. Her cheeks were flushed from the wind, and her hair stood out from her temples. She squinted.

"I lost my sunglasses," she said.

"You're crazy," I told her, and was envious the way I am of un-self-conscious people.

When I let her out at the airport, she hugged me and kissed my cheek.

"Be good," she told me.

She walked into the terminal without looking back, rolling a small suitcase, the cardboard tube tucked under her arm.

21

How strange, to love a city. Or a building. A rock, a tree, a river.

What a waste. Loving things that will never love you back. A painting. What a waste to love a painting. The wind. You can't even paint the wind.

But how much safer was it, Georgia, to love the desert. Safer to love a stone than a human. A stone may never love you back, but it will never love another. The desert never understands you, but it never misunderstands, either.

When I returned from the airport I saw that Omar had called, but I didn't call him back. There was a blank canvas on my easel. I looked at it for a long time, until my eyes swam with spots.

A color is a decision, but white is only waiting.

22

I realized the great losses born from my decision. On one hand, there was the loss of Georgia. I would never see her paintings again from a place of innocence and wonder. Her work was besmirched for me now, it was associated with my dishonesty and envy. I idolized her, she was a mentor, and somehow I'd betrayed her, taken advantage of the purity of her lines. I coveted what she had, and in my coveting had destroyed it for myself. This is part of what I had wanted to say to Maya the night before, but didn't quite know how to explain.

The second loss, which I could never have predicted, was the loss of the small nuclear friendship that had been forming between Maya, Jake, and me. I am by nature a solitary person, but since coming to Santa Fe I'd integrated others into my life. I liked them, admired them, was comfortable in their company. The imitations had forged a strong and necessary tie between Maya and me, but had also driven a wedge between me and Jake. When the three of us were together now, I was always aware of the tight, taut, secret string tying me to Maya. Jake was outside, excluded and protected. I imagine that Maya too must have felt the pressure of her duplicity, but she always seemed natural.

All this is an attempt to justify what happened next, because, you see, we were already broken.

A few days after Maya left, Jake was waiting for me in the museum lobby after work. He asked if I wanted to go see the opera house, he had some business to discuss with the manager. We walked together through the too-tall museum doors.

The opera house nestles on a hill on the outskirts of the city. I had never seen it before. It is a building that is not a building, with parts of ceilings and parts of walls. The north and south sides are open. On rainy nights, the people seated on the sides get wet. Four enormous sails stand on the south patio to block the wind. Poles like metal masts, and curving metal sails that turn silently in the breeze. The roof spreads like a seashell fan, and the stage is open in back onto the desert, rolling mounds of juniper-spotted dirt.

While Jake was speaking to the manager, I stood alone in the middle of the empty hall. It was like being in the middle of the ocean during a storm, the hills swelling around me like waves that are too deep to break.

A narrow moat of water separated the audience from the orchestra pit. I walked down the stairs and dipped my fingers in as if it were holy water, then I leaned over to peer down at the orchestra pit. It was painted completely black, with black chairs and black music stands and black curtains obscuring the black doors from which the musicians emerged. Black to make them invisible, as if the music condensed from air.

I didn't notice that the house lights were on until they blinked off, then I knew it was evening. Jake was standing by me in the partial light, his fingers trailing in the moat and his tattoo panther clambering up his arm away from the water.

"Do you want to go backstage?" he asked.

We walked below the stage, through the costume workshop, lit by bare bulbs. Half-made ball gowns adorned headless dummies, shimmering fish-scale cloth and bridal lace lay out haphazardly on cutting tables. Parts of sets were pushed against the walls, roman pillars wrapped in silk ivy, an enormous plywood guillotine.

The orchestra pit seemed too small to house so many people, enough people to play an entire opera. The theater was hushed with the ghosts of chorus girls and prima donnas, dancers and conductors and iron-lunged oboists, bassoonists, clarinetists. Jake leapt up the steps to the conductor's stand.

"Come up here."

I stood beside him. If I lifted my head, I could see across the dusty floor of the stage to the mountains, rolling like reclining bodies. The sun had already set.

"This is my other life," he said. "Now you know all of me."

"I'm getting old," he said.

"You're not old."

"I have grey hair."

"I like your grey hairs," I said. "I love your grey hairs."

"Getting older," he said, "it's just a gradual elimination of options."

"What?"

"You have so many choices right now," he said. "You can have Omar, you can be single, you can be a painter, you can go back to school, you can be a bum. See, choices."

"Like a life buffet," I suggested.

"Right, but you're the first one there, and I've been there too long, and it's all picked over."

"Anything I can do, you could do," I said.

"It's not the same."

"But even with all the choices, I still have to choose one thing," I said.

"I'm going to get old and regimented," Jake said. "Inflexible. I'm going to do the same thing every day at the same time."

"You won't if you don't want to," I said. "You don't ever have to do anything you don't want to do," I said again, not sure if it was true.

Jake picked up a pencil from the stand, cleared his throat and tapped it noisily. The sound startled me. He took a deep breath and spread his arms in the empty hall, as if he were conducting. Then he stopped and handed the pencil to me.

"You be the conductor," he said, and stepped down.

In the silence, I spread my arms like a stretching bird. Jake was below me now, and I was alone on the stand. He took a breath and began to sing, so I conducted.

We were laughing and then we were serious.

He did not sing words, or if he did I didn't understand them. I conducted high and he went to a thin falsetto. I conducted with big strokes and he sang a deep baritone. I conducted in tiny mouse movements, and he lowered his voice nearly to a whisper. Then I was still.

"It's a quiet ending," I said. "Tender." I placed the pencil back on the stand. The darkness came closer and the quiet was louder. Jake was a big black shadow in blackness.

"Should we go?" he asked.

"We should go," I said.

"We're going."

"Yes, we're going right now."

Back at the apartments it was dark. Jake went upstairs and I went downstairs. I listened as he moved above me. He was wearing heavy shoes and they thumped into the kitchen and out again. Then I heard the strains of a violin being tuned, the protestations of stretching strings. Slow scales trickled down to me, then faster, then arpeggios and a furious etude that cut off halfway through. Then his boots rang out of the apartment.

I opened my door before he knocked.

His fingers were gentle, I could feel their calluses on my face. When he kissed me, I smelled the rosin dust in his beard.

Sometimes it is two people in the same dark woods who never find each other, but only call out into silence. With us, it was two people who have found each other after many years, and walk together with the same stride, and forget where they are going because it doesn't matter. After a while you don't know who you are anymore.

I won't say any more, only that outside my window the city radiated its tiny streetlight glow into a vast night, the mountains lay all around us, and pine needles whispered far away.

Then Jake was asking, *Are you crying?*

I'm not crying, I said. He was kissing my eyelids and wiping tears from my cheeks.

Don't cry, he was saying, *please don't cry*, but my shoulders were shaking and I couldn't stop them.

23

Have I told you how blue the sky is in New Mexico? It is the bluest you've ever seen, a great blue dome. So blue and so distant that your eyes get confused. So blue you can only see your own eyes.

24

I went to the café the next morning, before my museum shift. Omar came from behind the counter and kissed my forehead. He always seemed happier in the mornings than the evenings, as if the passing of the day exhausted him.

After the morning rush passed, he joined me at the table where I'd been pretending to read the paper. I didn't know if I would tell him about Jake or not. Omar took the Arts section of the paper and glanced at the cover story about a local winemaker.

"Are you working on anything?" he asked.

"Something," I said.

"When do I get to see it?" he asked.

He was still looking at the photo of an older man with a denim button-down shirt stretched over his belly, hand resting proudly on a wine barrel.

"When it's perfect," I said.

Outside, birds twittered. The songbirds were lined up like soldiers in the morning, evenly spaced on the telephone wire across the street. I counted twelve birds. When one left, the remaining birds would all shift over to fill the space. They cast a shadow that was a swooping line broken by twelve, then eleven, perfectly spaced bumps.

"Are you okay?" Omar asked. He looked up from the paper.

If I were going to tell him something, though I didn't know what, this would be the time. I thought of the empty folding chair in the circle of students, all of them drawing air, waiting for the empty space to come together and form an answer.

"It's so nice out," I said. "We should open the door." And as Omar wedged a wooden block inside the door frame to let the morning in, I closed and locked a door inside of me.

The air was cool and gave me goosebumps on my arms, but it was cool in the way that precedes great heat; and you could smell the sun as it warmed the concrete and the asphalt and the rooftops and the still young leaves.

A man came in and ordered a vanilla latte. Omar made it, and then an espresso for himself. He prided himself on the clean brown foam on the top. He sat down with me again.

"Do you think Jake and Maya are going to get married?" I asked. I could say Jake's name because I had locked the door inside of me and didn't feel anything.

"I think Jake wants to," he said. "He doesn't like being alone."

"Not like you," I said.

Omar smiled. "I like being with you," he said.

Three birds flitted from the telephone wire to the sidewalk and tapped their beaks down to something I couldn't see.

"Do you think he loves her?" I asked.

Omar stirred his espresso gently, and spooned some of the foam off.

He said, "Jake feels safe when a woman loves him more than he loves her."

When it was time for me to go to work, Omar asked if he would see me that night.

"I can't," I said. "I have to paint."

But I didn't paint that night, because Jake came over, and the next night too.

As I lay there with Jake those nights I thought of how little we knew one another. We didn't speak of Maya then or Omar, we certainly didn't speak of love, nor did we explain or rationalize the inexplicable and irrational. His breaths were deeper than Omar's, he was more barrel-chested. I lay and wondered if I loved everyone or no one, and hoped I could keep all my lies straight. One lie makes another easier. The way that children learn to speak by speaking, one learns to lie by lying. At first there is a small voice inside of you saying, *what are you doing?* a small voice that is shocked and disappointed in you and dismayed that your moral compass has been so grossly misdirected. But you learn by ignoring to ignore the small voice. Or maybe sometimes you try to give an answer and there is none, just a resounding blank silence in you, and perhaps the small voice gets tired of the non-answer and goes away. Only I couldn't lie to Georgia, and as I walked farther in my life, I felt her eluding me, I knew her less and less. With her I felt the way you can't look someone in the eyes and lie to them. Before, I could imagine her silent ghost as a mentor or even a guardian angel, but she had abandoned me now, she regarded me with disdain. I could no longer imagine her face. She turned her back to me.

25

The day before Maya returned from New York, Jake and I went to the river. The Rio Grande does not run by Santa Fe, but we drove to where it does run, by a narrow winding road where people drive too fast. He pulled off the road and we parked on a wide dirt shoulder.

The river rambled and bumped at the bottom of the cliff. We scrambled over scree and loose boulders to get down, grasping at weeds for balance. My palms were scraped and raw at the bottom. Jake leapt out and landed on a boulder a few feet from the shore. I stood unsure, my feet buried in the deep sticky mud.

The Rio Grande is neither blue nor clear, but a thick muddy grey-brown. The surface is never liquid smooth, but rippled from all the underwater obstacles, branches and rocks, tires, car parts, fish hooks, beer cans. It is not a river for swimming. I watched the river eddy around my calves. The movement of the water made me dizzy.

This land was Jake's home. He and Omar had grown up here, among the cottonwoods. Maya and I were the transplants, the intruders. I'd asked Omar once about growing up with Jake, and he'd said, simply, *Jake was always everyone's favorite.*

I joined him on the boulder and the water swirled around us, thick as paint. The stone was warm, and two water spots spread from my feet and then evaporated. Jake was talking about his childhood, growing up in the mountains with dirt roads and cocaine deals and heartbreaking sunsets.

"My old man's a carpenter," he told me. "He built our house."

I imagined him as a child in a small sunny house filled with his mother's looms and skeins of dyed wool. His door, I was sure, would be painted blue.

"I'd like to build my own house," I told him.

We sat like sentries on the boulder, arms around our knees, our shoulders touching. The cliff on the other side of the river, across from the road, was even steeper. The rock looked crumbly and weeds grew in the cracks.

Jake picked at loose gravel from a crack in the boulder. He threw pebbles into the river one by one. Each one disappeared with a different pitch. He asked me if I loved Omar.

I thought of Omar, the line that appeared between his eyebrows when he was worried and disappeared when he was looking for birds.

"No," I said. "No, I don't think so." He tossed three pebbles at the same time and I watched them hit the water with tiny ripples, *plink plink plunk*. "Are you in love with Maya?"

He squinted down the river.

"Yes, I guess I am," he said finally. His face was tan from years spent in the sun and wind. Fine lines radiated from his eyes, sunspots freckled his cheekbones.

"She's a strong woman, Ivy," he told me.

I nodded.

We were very hidden, on the river in the canyon. The sun was still high, but the shadow of the cliff on the other side had begun to creep across the water towards us. The sky was blue and unbearable.

"No clouds today," I said after awhile.

"No," Jake agreed. "No clouds."

When the shadow caught up to us, we left the river and scrambled back to the car, pebbles sliding in our wake.

26

When I was with Jake I never thought about Omar, and
with Omar I tried not to think about Jake; and no matter
whom I was with, I tried not to think about Georgia. When I
was alone I thought about everyone, until they all cancelled
one another out, the way all the colors together make white
light. This is the way we compartmentalize our lives. I clas-
sified myself into different boxes, like Linnaeus categorizing
all his different plants. Broad-leafed deciduous trees distinct
from the fine-needled pines, separate organisms sprung from
the same ground. They interact only in happenstantial ways.

This is the way we understand our contradictions, through
separation and classification. I've always been mistrustful of
people who harbor no contradictions. They are either lying
to themselves or lying to me. My father was the contradiction of an atheist theologist; he took faith and examined it
at an arm's length, dispassionately, as the faithful never do.
My mother's contradiction was in the split of her time, her
mind working in eons and mega-centuries, a scale where
mountain ranges form and crumble like tides coming in and
out; a scale of twenty-four hours where human beings only
appeared in the last second of the last minute before mid-
night, a scale she balanced skillfully with the everyday world
where coffee boils over and eggs go bad.

On my hardest days, I return to my parents' cool rationality. The days when I see someone I love, and it makes
the marrow of my bones ache because it is never enough to
love, because what I really want is to dissolve myself into

them. Not just an awkward coupling of limbs, but a complete fusing of breastbones, femurs, and ribs that will not be undone after a desperate, clawing hour. On these hardest of days, I try to remember that lives have been cycling in and out of suffering and desire for as long as I could dream. And even that cycling is tiny in comparison with the splittings and groanings and molten explosions that periodically rock this earth.

Some days this comforts me more than other days.

27

Jake went alone to pick Maya up from the airport. I pulled a stool to my window and sat with my feet on the ledge. The phone rang but I didn't answer. I watched the sky turn from blue to lavender to grey to a darkness that has no color. I stayed until the headlights of Jake's truck swung across the street and I heard their voices in the hall, climbing the stairs. I thought maybe Maya would come by, but she didn't.

The door upstairs closed.

The next day, Maya and I walked towards the plaza.

"You're brilliant," she told me. "They loved you."

It was a week day. There were not many people out. Sullen kids, just out of school for the summer, smoked cigarettes by the statue in the plaza. A young mother with her daughter sitting on a park bench.

Maya and I sat on another bench. It was not comfortable, green trellised-iron.

"Eric has two collectors that he thinks will be interested," Maya said. "The third painting he'll probably put in an auction house. He'll wire us money as soon as they sell. It should be less than two months."

It was strange hearing Maya speak about this. She seemed to be talking from someplace very far away about something very remote. Her chin jutted into a fine point. I thought about what Jake had said about Maya being a strong woman. For a moment, despite myself, I imagined Jake's hands cupping her chin.

The girl left her mother's side and began walking on the curb between the plaza and the street, her arms outstretched for balance. Her hair was pulled back in a ponytail.

"Ivy, do you want to do this?" Maya asked me.

"Yes." I said.

"Are you sure? Because I need you to be sure. Don't do this because I want you to. It's your decision." She was serious, and seemed older. I told her I was sure.

"Why?" she asked. "Tell me why." Her legs were crossed at the ankles, tucked beneath the bench. I was leaning forward, elbows on knees. The ponytailed girl reached the end of the curb, turned around.

"Jesus, Maya. I don't know."

"Yes you do. Tell me why you want to do this."

The tree shadows all had full summer leaves. They shook over the sidewalk. The streets around the plaza are not paved but brick, uneven and poking up. A policeman on a tall horse with a shining brown coat sauntered by, cast a glance towards the smoking kids, who pretended to ignore him. Horse hooves clicked on the bricks, the ankles knobby. I realized that I had no idea why I did anything.

"Do you think she was satisfied?" I asked.

"Who?"

"Georgia. Do you think she finished a painting and thought, yes, this is what I wanted to say; or do you think she finished and thought, maybe the next one will be better?"

Maya took a deep breath. She seemed to be exercising great patience with me. "I don't know," she said.

The girl on the curb stopped and looked up at the policeman. Her eyes were solemn and round. He tipped his hat at her, but she didn't respond.

"I guess I'm jealous," I tried to say this lightly. "I just want to do something I like."

28

I'd expected that when Maya was in town, I would only see Jake at work; but one afternoon and then another, and then so many afternoons I lost count, we drove partway up the ski hill to a small dirt pullout. When Jake snapped the engine off, the wind carried sounds of the city up to the mountains, horns and stereos and trucks downshifting. Then the wind changed direction and we could only hear leaves rustling.

He would look at me with his eyes a question. Funny, I thought, that we can see questions in eyes—a small change in color, the pupils slightly larger or slightly smaller, a tensing or relaxing in the myriad of fine muscles around the sockets. How would I begin to paint that instinctive question? Shadows of full-leaved aspens and firs spotted the windshield and spilled onto our skin.

"Should we talk about this?" he asked one afternoon.

"I don't know," I said. "I don't understand it."

Particles of dust floated in the back of the truck, the high dirty windows open and clicked into place. "I feel like I'm in high school," Jake said. "I feel so young." He laughed. Aspen leaves hit one another and pine needles brushed pine needles. There was the sound of a car downshifting around the corner behind us.

"Why do you look so sad?" Jake asked. With my fingers I traced the outline of a stain on the blanket, shaped like a continent on a map, seashore on all the edges. The human being smell of us wafted out the windows. I imagined our scent riding and curling and dissipating like smoke through the trees.

"I don't feel young," I said to the roof of his truck. Then I turned to look at him, and his face was only an inch from mine. I could see the few grey hairs at his temples and every pore in his nose.

Jake smiled. "But you're just a baby," he said, not unkindly.

I twisted my arm around to hold his head from the back, my fingers around his skull. I liked the weight of it. He had one protrusion in the back, a lump that you couldn't see but could feel. The first time I'd touched it, I'd asked him if it hurt and he feigned pain—then laughed when I was alarmed and apologized.

"Do you ever feel like you're not doing anything important?" I asked.

"Now you sound like Omar," Jake said. "You'll grow out of that."

"I'm serious," I said. "What are we doing with our lives?"

"Making love," Jake said. He rolled over on his side so we were facing each other, nose to nose. "I'm serious, too. You can aspire and analyze and philosophize until you die, but it doesn't matter."

I took a breath and then exhaled to watch all the dust move in the sunlight.

"It just doesn't matter," he repeated.

In the evenings, my skin smelled like Jake's skin and I took showers to wash him from me. In different rooms in the same building we washed each other from ourselves. Hot water swished up the pipes in my walls to the shower above my own, and then my skin cells rinsed off of Jake and Jake's skin cells rinsed off of me, and they rolled down the drain and met somewhere below the building, in cooling soapy water.

I continued to see Omar and it became easier to lie. What all liars know is that to lie, you have to believe the lie

94

yourself. So when Omar asked what I was doing after work, I could say I was painting and almost believe it myself, even as I stepped up into Jake's truck, even as I put my feet up on his dashboard, even as I pulled his face into my neck. And when Omar reached for me in the nights and put the tapered fingers I had so admired over my hips, I could believe that I pushed him away because I was very, very tired. And when Maya brought me bread she'd made and smiled when she told me something Jake had said, I could smile back and listen and believe that I wanted the best for Maya and Jake, I could almost believe that I wasn't jealous. I could almost believe that I wanted him to love her more.

29

I spent my days at the museum leafing through gift books and thinking about the next O'Keeffe painting I would do. My sketchbooks began to fill with shadowed drawings of bones and hills.

As spring dried to summer, grass turned into brown confetti and fires seemed to start out of wind. It was going to be a bad fire season, said the news, and every day they announced where new hungry fires were. In the Pecos, in the Jemez, tearing through dry ponderosas, gobbling pine needles, jumping from the crowns of trees over dirt roads and ditches. Flames higher than buildings, great plumes of acrid smoke that you could taste when the wind blew your way. In the nights, you could look to the mountains in the west and see an orange glow. With binoculars you could see the spark of individual flames.

Everyone was talking about the fires. People whose homes were in the area were evacuated and came to Santa Fe. Hotels let evacuated families stay for half price and made exceptions to pet rules, allowing dogs, cats, hamsters, rabbits, iguanas, carried in cages by wide-eyed children, who didn't know if their homes were at that minute collapsing to a charred pile, glass melting like candy, reforming in gravity-twisted shapes.

Omar and I were sitting on folding chairs on my roof one night watching the distant glow of fires. The rooftop was flat, covered with tar and rough gravel that crunched beneath the chairs when I shifted my weight. Below us, the light was on in Jake and Maya's kitchen. A rectangle of light shone from their window into the alley behind the building. From the hard-packed dirt the rectangle of light bent up suddenly and climbed partway up the adobe wall. I could see the unevenness of the adobe that I hadn't noticed before.

"Did you ever want to be a firefighter?" I asked.

"Not so much," Omar said.

A tinkling peal of laughter rose like smoke from Jake and Maya's window, then after a brief pause, more laughter, this time with Jake's deep baritone chiming in.

"They're so happy," said Omar.

"They are," I said.

"Like us," he said.

He stood up and came to where I was sitting. Lifted my face to see him, outlined by starlight. He kissed me very, very gently.

Crickets chirped from someplace nearby.

"Just like us," I said.

Gravel crackled as he sat back down. I looked out towards the burning mountains, eerie and silent in destruction.

"Do you mind?" Omar took a packet of rolling paper from his chest pocket.

"I used to want to be a firefighter," I said, watching him.

"You?" He looked amused.

Omar pinched the fine strands of tobacco into the paper balanced on his knee. He folded it lovingly, concentrating in the dim light from the corner streetlamp. His fingers were long, smooth-knuckled.

"You have musician's fingers," I told him.

"They're just waiter's hands," he said.

I traced his profile with my eyes. Temple, cheekbone, jaw. He brought the rolled cigarette to his mouth, licked it to seal it, inspected his work. When he struck the match behind his cupped hand, I saw the flame reflected in both his eyes. He shook out the match and dropped it, exhaled white smoke into the streetlamp light.

"So you're going to be a firefighter," he said. "What kinds of fires will you fight?"

"The bad ones," I said.

"You'll let the good ones burn?"

"I'll only fight forest fires," I said. "I'll let the cities burn."

He ground his shoe again over the fading match. Another cricket joined in the choir.

"What about people's houses?" he asked.

"Let them burn," I said.

"Even mine?"

"Sorry."

A shadow moved in Jake and Maya's window. I couldn't tell if it was a man or a woman.

"What about the café?"

"You've got insurance," I said.

There was no moon that night, only winking burning stars over our winking burning planet.

"Imagine," I said in the cricket-song. "All of Santa Fe streaming up flames, gas stations exploding. Suddenly you have nothing. It would be liberating, everything you have is gone. You'd start everything over fresh, like a little baby."

"I've already done it," Omar said. "Once was enough."

He took a deep drag from his cigarette and held it for a full ten seconds before exhaling. He was looking straight at me the whole time.

"And what will you do, Miss Firefighter, while your home is burning?"

"I'll stand on the top of Baldy," I said, "and paint it all in great fiery strokes."

Jake and Maya's light switched off, and the dirt-packed alley disappeared. There was the almost-silent pad of feline feet on the adobe wall, then a high-pitched squeak and I could see the erratic black movement of a bat zigzagging, hunting gnats in the starlight. Omar flicked ash onto the gravel.

"What about the museum?" he asked.

I watched the bat dive in small circles, reflecting his sonar voice off tiny dust-speck victims. The air smelled of night and fire.

"Let it burn," I said.

He laughed, a short puff, and leaned over to grind his cigarette into the gravel.

"Some firefighter," he said.

30

By the middle of June, the days were long. Mornings were cool and smoky and dry, and by ten o'clock a still dry heat sat over the plaza and not even the cottonwood leaves wanted to move. Always the smell of ponderosas burning somewhere. It was not the kind of heat that makes you sweat, but the kind that drinks you dry.

I didn't mind the heat as I walked towards Omar's apartment. In the distance, a few billowing thunderheads gathered around the Jemez Mountains. Clouds had begun to gather each afternoon, building from the mountaintops and blowing over the city. Still, there was no rain. The clouds built and billowed and strained and arched their backs, and then trickled away like seeds spreading in the wind. They would swell, blue-bottomed, and stir up winds, and dry leaves would rattle a rain dance, but still no rain. There was a sense of waiting, the anticipation of rain born each morning and frustrated with each scattering of clouds.

Omar didn't answer when I knocked. I tried the door half-heartedly and was surprised when it opened. His curtains were drawn over open windows, and stirred slightly at the disturbance of a door opening into a still room. My eyes took a moment to adjust to the darkness. The apartment was an island of shady coolness in the sun-blinded city. His walls seemed slightly dirty, as if from all the years of collecting oils and cooking smells from the air.

I heard a sigh, and walked towards his bedroom. From the doorway, I saw Omar sleeping on his back with one arm sprawled out beside him. The top button of his shirt was undone and the shirttails were untucked. His lips were slightly parted in sleep, and his chest moved steadily as he breathed. Beside his bed, his shoes were set neatly side by side. He needed a haircut, and somehow looked vulnerable, sleeping in the afternoon.

He was at that moment more beautiful than I remembered. I didn't think I loved him, but he had cheekbones carved from smooth dark wood. I liked to see that face change beneath me, to see him close his eyes.

I didn't want to disturb him, and wandered back into the living room to wait for him to wake up.

The only decoration in the apartment was a framed poster he had gotten from a garage sale, of Spanish moss hanging from cypress trees in the Florida Keys. The moss hung like curtains, almost touching the knobby cypress knees that emerged from the swamp. The living room opened into his kitchen. A dull pea-green refrigerator harbored a few alphabet magnets left by the last tenant, a purple L and an orange B. Through the curtains, from the open window, wafted the clanging sounds of construction a few blocks away, the slam of hammers and grunting of machinery.

I was suddenly aware of us all. Of Jake, on the outskirts of town now, tuning his violin, the chin rest smooth against his beard. And Maya with him, on the other side of the conductor, cello cradled amidst her skirts; and Omar asleep a hundred feet from where I was, with his ankles crossed and his smooth neck. And I thought about how full of contradictions we are, always wanting two different things at the same time, and believing two different things at the same time; and all our different ideas bouncing around inside of us, bumping into each other. Maya seemed so sure of herself all the time, seemed to know what to do without questioning. Whatever I did seemed like a lie to somebody. It was as though I were living not one life but several, with a growing abyss between each. Like a landscape carved by a web of rivers that never meet, so many isolated mesas. Each person I knew was a witness to a different life; my life with Maya distinct from my life with Jake, which in turn was distinct and isolated from my life with Omar. All three lives separate from the true private life I lived in my apartment. All these different sides of me viewed the others from a distance with a vague, impersonal curiosity. They considered one another from the tops of separate mesas in a sunny desert, occasionally lifting a hand in greeting but out of shouting range.

I thought I would wake Omar after all, or maybe just lie down by him until our breathing matched.

As I was standing up from the couch, I noticed a manila envelope that had slipped between the cushions. It looked like the envelope Maya had given me with the painting close-ups. The flap was unsealed and open, and I saw the edges of photographs. I hesitated only a moment before taking them out. There were three photos, eight by eleven glossy prints of paintings. On the back of each, someone had written a date with a black pen in small, neat handwriting. The date was the day before Maya had gone to New York.

They were photographs of my paintings, three slightly different views of the Ranchos de Taos church.

I knew, suddenly, that Omar was the photographer. Omar, who liked to make love in the afternoons, who kissed my knuckles one by one. He had known all along that I was doing the forgeries, had probably told Maya about the first painting he'd seen in my apartment the first night we met. Omar, who was probably making a profit from my work.

I was standing there with the photos in my hand when Omar appeared in the doorway. He had been re-tucking his shirt, but was frozen with the tails still half out. His hair was rumpled from sleep. His eyes were fixed on mine. At the corners of his eyes, his eyelashes were tangled, the upper lashes caught with the lower.

We stood like this for a long time, impossibly long. The silence inside was magnified by the noise of a distant hammer. He parted his lips once and took a breath as if to speak, but remained silent. I felt the skin around my eyes tighten. I looked at him as if I'd never seen him before and saw again how dark his eyes were, almost black. For the first time, I saw not a serious, beautiful man, but an individual with a past, with his own impenetrable inner life. I looked at him and suddenly knew that he, too, harbored an entire world that I would never know.

I set the photographs on the coffee table as gently as I could, but the sound was sharp as lightning.

Still Omar said nothing, still we looked at one another, unsmiling. We eyed each other like two animals—testing, challenging, cowering. It became apparent that he was waiting for me to speak. I took a breath.

"Did you sleep well?" I said.

"You're angry," he said.

What some people would have said is, *Yes, I'm angry. Of course I'm angry, you've been lying to me since the day we met*; and what I should have said is, *I'm done, I'm out, take your insincerity and plotting and using each other and leave me alone.*

But what I said was, "Maybe."

Omar swore. He ran both his hands through his hair. Then stormed into his room and came back with his cell phone.

I wanted to walk out his door, down the steps into the fading afternoon and never turn around, walk into the foothills and the mountains and keep on. But when I moved towards the door, Omar shouted, *don't leave*, and for some reason I didn't.

"I don't care," he was saying into the phone. "You have to explain it to her."

Somewhere beyond the curtain and the darkened room, someone was building something. I heard the hammer falling, knocking the nail and then the wood and then a pause, and I imagined the builder taking the next nail from his pocket, or perhaps from between his teeth, positioning it gently.

"I don't care," Omar was saying. "Right now."

I sat on his thrift store couch, sank into the cushions. The weight of my own blindness and stupidity pushed me down further. It was exactly what I deserved, I thought.

Omar snapped his phone shut and sat beside me. He pressed the heel of his hand against his forehead.

"Please don't look at me like that," he said.

"How am I supposed to look at you?" I asked.

The cranes sounded as if they were lifting a great weight, steel beams. A cement mixer was grinding its steady mud.

"Don't put your arm around me," I said.

"Maya's coming over," he said.

I looked at the magnets on his refrigerator and thought about what they could stand for. Lost Baby. Beautiful Liar. You could fold the B horizontally across the middle and it was symmetrical. No symmetry in L. The shape of the B somehow evoked the way lips touch to say it.

"Please say something," Omar said.

"Did you take these?" I asked, even though I knew that he had. "These and the other pictures that Maya gave me?"

Omar said nothing, but looked down at his feet. He hadn't put his shoes back on after his nap, and the bones of his feet angled in sharp geometry beneath his socks.

"Why didn't you tell me?" I asked.

"I wanted to be open from the beginning," Omar said. "But Maya thought it was better to wait."

I remembered our most tender moments, touching noses and soft exhalations, and thought how we were both lying, how dishonest and contrived our intimacy had been. How false everything was.

"I know what you think," he said.

I said, "You have no idea what I think."

I stood up from the couch and went to stand by the window. I pulled aside the curtains with one hand and let the sun shock my eyes. His apartment was eye-level with the powerlines, and there were no trees on his street. I couldn't understand why Maya hadn't told me that Omar was the photographer; although once I knew it was him, it was obvious. Suddenly, Omar had gone from lover to business partner. Only he'd known all along that we were business partners. Birds settled on the power lines, chirped their protest to the heat, and sought shadier perches. I let the curtain drop and looked back at Omar, who was still leaning his elbows on his knees and holding his head with both hands, his hair sticking out between his fingers.

I didn't ask if Maya had told him to sleep with me.

"You've been planning to sell my paintings since you first came to my apartment," I accused.

Omar looked up, raising his eyebrows and wrinkling his forehead. "You're talented," he said. "You know that."

"Do you even like my work?" I asked. "Do you even like me? Or are you and Maya just going to make a profit?"

Omar exhaled loudly and put his head back in his hands.

Anger, too, has a color, and this was blue, center-of-the-flame anger. Other people's anger, the kind they wear on their faces and in their voices, is outer-flame lashing orange-yellow anger. People who grew up in big families with brothers and sisters and cousins get angry this way. The outer-flame anger is when we hurt each other, but then we heal. My anger was different, and I didn't want to share it; it made me cold, and the desert canyon between us widened.

Then Maya came in. She opened the door without knocking. She must have hurried to get here from her rehearsal, but she appeared unruffled, her face was composed. She carried a bottle of wine, and her bracelets jingled merrily as she closed the door.

"You both look so serious," she said to Omar and me.

The envelope and three photos were on the coffee table. Maya picked them up, smoothly slid the photos back into the envelope.

"Well," she said.

She held up the bottle of wine. "Three glasses? I was going to tell you, Ivy, that Omar is helping us out."

"So why didn't you?"

"I am. I'm telling you right now." She walked into the kitchen and opened a drawer, closed it, and returned to the living room with a corkscrew and three mismatched wine glasses. Omar and I watched as she broke the seal easily with the point of the corkscrew. She threaded the corkscrew into the cork, pulled it out with a quiet pop. I could see the tendons in Maya's neck. Her hair was pulled back loosely, with a few strands straying over her shoulder.

"Helping out," I repeated. Outside, the noise of the hammers had stopped, and I thought that the workers must be going home for the day.

Maya poured the wine against the side of the glasses so it didn't splash. Omar wasn't looking at either of us, but was focusing on the glasses. He lifted one and tilted it so the wine almost spilled out, looking through the liquid.

"You should be able to read a newspaper through a good white wine," he observed.

"He helps out with the money," Maya told me. She swirled her glass and held it beneath her nose. "Where else would we put the money but in a business bank account? And you know how we benefit from his photography. I'm sorry I didn't bring it up earlier, but honestly, Ivy, it's not that important. It shouldn't change anything."

She drank her wine very calmly. The first breeze of the day nudged at the bottom of Omar's curtains.

"So we're all business partners," I said, and my voice was center-of-the-flame steady and revealed nothing.

"As long as we're all here," Maya said, as if everything had been satisfactorily resolved, "the word from Eric is that two clients are definitely in. He'll sell the third painting at an auction house, which is a little riskier, but we've had success there in the past."

"In the past," I repeated. Maya and Omar looked at each other.

"I don't want to know," I said.

Omar refilled his glass and Maya's, and refilled the few sips I'd taken from mine. Maya's lipstick had left a faint, striated smudge on her glass.

"He'd also be interested in any other paintings you could give him," Maya addressed me directly. "I told him I'd see if I couldn't squeeze a couple more out of you."

The wine was cold, and a damp fog had appeared on each glass. My hands absorbed the coldness of the wine.

"Does Jake know?" I asked.

"Jake doesn't need to know anything," Maya said.

Omar had his hand on my knee.

Maya leaned back in her chair and crossed her legs. She bounced her leg up and down casually in her flat sandals and smiled.

"Don't be mad. That goes for you, too, Omar. There's nothing to be upset at. Come on. Let's drink. Isn't this good wine? Perfect for an afternoon. To Georgia."

The three of us clinked glasses. The wine was crisp and smooth, and left a sweet dryness in my throat; and as they toasted Georgia, I toasted my own new alone-ness.

31

Outside the house is an enormous old ponderosa, and beneath the ponderosa is a wooden bench where Georgia would lie. In the day she lay, and the sky was blue and dizzying, defined by the branches that radiated out above her. At night the sky was broken into the same shapes by the same branches, and the same needles rustled against each other, but the smell was different. In the day the ponderosa smells of warm vanilla butterscotch, muted by dust and pine needles. At night the coolness is sudden. It makes the air seem less dry, and awakens dark woody odors in the cracked bark. She lay there for hours and watched the different shades of red pass over the bark with the sun. When it is windy, the far branches rock with patient grace. When it is still, they are only waiting. She lay beneath the tree outside the house that would be famous, where famous writers lived and famous socialites visited. She lay there when she was alone and listened to the roar of an empty sky. Sometimes she lay there when there were visitors inside the house, and then the night was softened by a bright light from the windows, and the clink of glasses inside tamed the roaring silence.

32

Once you admit to yourself that you want to be an artist, that you want nothing more in your life than to paint, you've taken a great weight upon your shoulders. Or maybe you acknowledge a need that can only be appeased by painting. Always following you, inescapable as a part of your body, is the nagging sensation that you should be working, you should be painting. Suddenly everything else in your life becomes an obstacle, keeping you from your only duty, which is to paint.

Before I'd painted the first real O'Keeffe forgery, making copies just as an exercise for myself had quieted that persistent ache. But once I was no longer doing it solely for myself, it became simply another distraction from my own work. As pleased as I was by the quality of the Ranchos paintings, I was unsettled the whole time by the idea that I wasn't really working.

I was thinking about this one hot day when Maya and I were lying on the floor of my apartment. It was too hot outside to move. The wood floor was cool, and we lay with our arms spread wide as if to make snow angels. This was the thing about Maya, she always seemed so comfortable that it made you comfortable, too. And despite everything, despite the sudden knowledge that Omar was part of it, despite the part of me that felt tricked somehow, and the larger, more insistent part of me that knew I was being a bad friend to Maya, despite all that I felt, at moments like this, that we were close.

Besides, I thought, you are never completely honest with anyone, no matter how much you love them.

I told Maya I was worried that I wasn't working on my own paintings anymore.

"Maybe you need someplace else to work," she said. "Separate places for your separate kinds of painting."

I thought about this. Maybe I had gotten too close, confused the forgeries for art. If I could work on them someplace else, they would be just another job, like working at the museum, to supplement my real work. Maya said that Omar's grandparents had a bunkhouse north of Abiquiu that I might be able to use.

The sun had shifted since she'd come over, and now it reached through the window in a long rectangle and landed on my feet. I lay for a moment feeling the heat, then turned to be in the shade again.

"Are you mad about Omar?" Maya asked.

I bent one knee up and felt the cool wooden floor on the bottom of my foot. I tried to weigh Maya's question in my heart. I looked for anger, but didn't feel any.

"I don't understand why you didn't tell me before," I said.

I turned my head without lifting it to look at her. My ear pressed against the floor and over my outstretched arm I could see her hair pooling around her head. I closed one eye and she disappeared behind my hand. I could block her whole face out just by lifting my fingers. Then I closed the other eye and she reappeared. She was not going to respond to this.

"Do you want kids?" she asked.

I turned my head back up to regard the ceiling again. That peeling paint chip in the corner.

"I don't know who I'd have them with," I said.

"I used to want five," she said.

"Five?" I said. The floor hard on my skull at two points. I wondered if my skull was oddly misshapen.

"What happened?" I asked after awhile. "You changed your mind?"

"I'm thirty-three, Ivy," she said, and then didn't say anything for awhile.

Before she left she said again that she would talk to Omar about using his grandparents' bunkhouse.

"It's probably a good idea not to have all the evidence in your apartment, anyway," she said. I nodded, though the word *evidence* left a strangely metallic flavor in my mouth.

The drive up to the bunkhouse was the same road north I'd taken in the spring, past Ghost Ranch and Echo Amphitheater. Omar and I left in the morning, but the day was already warming, and it would be hot. The whole world seemed thirsty as we left town. New fires had blossomed in the south, and even in the morning the air had a faint taste of smoke.

We didn't speak as we left town. I looked out the window at the small flat-roofed houses with blighted lawns and chain-linked backyards. Dogs barked from one side of a house, then ran behind it to bark from the other as we passed. St. Francis Drive was strung with dusty gas stations and impersonal fast food joints and sterile office buildings behind high walls. In the side mirror I watched the yellow stripe on the side of the road, racing into the past so quickly that it didn't seem to move at all.

Omar drove with one hand, guiding the steering wheel from the bottom. He kept his window cracked open, smoked cigarettes and tapped the ash out the window.

As we drove further north, there were no other cars on the road. There seemed to be nobody else in the world, only hills and cliffs, and occasionally the river would come into view. Always the blue peaks and mounds of the mountains in the distance.

"I can see why she was inspired," I said.

Omar snorted. "Inspiration," he said. "Is that what they taught you in art school?"

I had my feet up on the dashboard, my knees bent to my chest. He glanced over but didn't say anything, so I left my feet where they were.

"Because it's bullshit," Omar continued.

"The art world," he pronounced, "isn't about art. It's about knowing the right people, knowing how to talk about your art."

The road curved around and began to climb a short hill. Omar and I reached up at the same time to adjust the visors, blocking the sun from our eyes.

Omar continued. "It helps if you have something that appeals to people on some basic level," he said, "but you have to be able to justify it. In words."

Since I'd learned that Omar and Maya were working in tandem, a slight change had occurred in our relationship. We were the same, but through a different colored filter. Or perhaps without a filter at all, but with all illusions and pretenses stripped off. In bed we used our teeth more, and we bit harder. We were hostile the way that people who can take one another's love for granted are hostile. Except what we took for granted was that we were stuck together in this messy deception.

"Do you think O'Keeffe would have been anything without Steiglitz?" he was saying. "He saw something in her—and frankly I'm not even sure it was the art—and he *made* her. Without his gallery, she'd have been another old maid school teacher in Texas."

I took my feet off the dashboard and sat up in the seat. The road curved again, and I raised the sun visor.

"Maybe she wouldn't have gotten the recognition," I said, "but she still would have been painting." Omar glanced in the rearview mirror, and then at me.

"And she probably would have been just as happy," I said.

112

We passed through a tiny town, just a gas station and a restaurant and a general store. I could tell by the trees that we were gaining elevation. There were no more junipers, and fewer cottonwoods. Instead we passed heavier pines and occasionally a cluster of aspens.

"I'm not saying she wasn't a brilliant painter," Omar said. "I'm just saying it takes more than vision, it takes connections."

"Depends on your definition of success," I said, and rolled my window down all the way.

The bunkhouse is a one-room cottage that Jake and Omar's grandparents had built to house ranch hands who used to come and help out seasonally. It has a split-level roof, and at the top of a steep handmade staircase, a small loft for sleeping. The south wall is made of rough muddy bricks, with pieces of straw still poking out. A potbellied woodburning stove stands in the middle of the room with a chimney that extends through the roof and radiates heat throughout the bunkhouse. Boards clamped to the walls serve as shelves and cupboards. They hold chipped plates and empty mason jars used as drinking glasses. On the top shelves, old tins for coffee and maple syrup, glass bottles, two smoky kettles. By the single window is a handmade table and three wooden chairs. Vases with spindly dried flowers and herbs. Hooks on the wall with a cast- iron skillet, a ladle, pots and pans. A rack of deer horns used to hold several cowboy hats and an old, sweat-stained trucker cap. Also on the walls, two pairs of old-fashioned wooden snowshoes strung with rawhide, a worn brown rope, a tarnished trumpet. By the stove, a stack of firewood and an old phone book to start the fires. Flannel shirts and down vests hung on the back of the door.

I don't know if Omar felt bad about our hostility on the drive up, or if he was comforted by childhood memories, but he seemed to soften when we were at the house. That afternoon, he took me to the woods where he and Jake had played as children.

"We used to build forts out here and try to make Indian traps for elk," he told me. "Every summer until my folks moved down to Santa Fe. Then I'd only get up here for a couple weeks. But by then Jake was older and running with a different group, anyway." Omar's father was a police officer, or a sheriff—I was never sure. I'd only met Omar's parents once, briefly and awkwardly. His father spoke in curt, unsmiling sentences, and his mother was a diminutive woman who looked baffled when I told her what my parents did.

Omar and I skirted low, marshy ground and walked where the grasses were shorter and the earth rockier. He took me to a group of aspen trees, and showed me the tree where he and Jake had carved their initials when they were younger. *JV. OV.* Jake Valdez. Omar Valdez. Jake being older and thus taller when they'd carved their initials, his were on top. The tree scars had grown in, dark and bulky, slightly distorting the letters and making them thick. To the right of Jake's initials, a smaller, younger cut read *MR* for Maya Rabini.

Jake was almost six years older than Omar, which had surprised me at first because Omar seemed older for his seriousness. It also surprised me because it made Jake thirty-six-years old, twelve years my senior.

Looking at his initials, I thought for a moment in spite of myself of the dark outline of Jake's shoulders above me, and how I had held his arms, above his elbows. To push away this sudden longing, I stood closer to Omar on the rocky, root-pierced ground. Above us, aspen leaves tinkled, smaller and higher pitched than the sound of cottonwoods.

"How is it that Jake doesn't know?" I asked. "About what you and Maya do."

Omar reached absentmindedly towards the tree and ran his fingers over Maya's initials.

"It's Maya," he said. "She has some notion about keeping Jake pure." Patches of sunlight flickered over his face as the wind blew.

"Since Jake stopped drinking, he has this weird aura," Omar searched for the right word. "Honorability or something."

I didn't want to think about Jake's honorability. I wanted to know more—what would Jake think of Maya suddenly having so much money, for example. Or would he even know. But Omar didn't seem to want to talk about it.

"Listen," he said, and cocked his head towards a high-pitched clicking above us, *pit-ik, pit-er-ik*. "A Western Tanager."

The bunkhouse had no electricity, and in the evening Omar lit three kerosene lanterns with thick wide wicks and glass tops curving like flowerbuds. We made a bright, popping fire in the stove, and boiled water for cooking and washing. We sat side by side on wooden chairs with our feet outstretched and crossed at the ankles. I felt at that moment that we were friends, that we understood one another. I was struck by this observation because it was probably the first time I'd really felt friendship with Omar. We had moved quickly, perhaps too quickly, into an intimacy fueled by mutual attraction. I watched the flames kicking against the glass panel on the tiny stove door, and wondered if Omar ever felt oppressed by his looks, the way I imagine beautiful women become defined by men's lust.

"Will you be able to paint here?" Omar asked over the noise of the girdled fire.

"It's perfect," I said.

The water on the top of the stove was boiling, but neither of us moved to take it off. Occasionally, a large bubble would splash over the edge, and hiss and steam up when it hit the metal. Omar used a black iron handle to open the door of the stove to put another rough log inside. A sweet trickle of smoke escaped into the room.

Looking into the open stove, Omar said, "Ivy, you know I want you to sell these paintings and make money as much as Maya does. We've sold a few smaller paintings through Eric, but you're our ticket." He stirred the orange embers and a few sparks flew out onto the bricks surrounding the stove.

"But don't let it stop you from doing your own painting. Don't let this work silence you."

He didn't look at me as he spoke, and I was startled at how closely he'd guessed my mind.

33

After that weekend, I spent most of my free time at the bunkhouse. I switched my schedule at the museum so that my days off were all in a row, and I would drive up in the evenings after my shift and stay two or three days at a time. Just before the turn-off onto the dirt road was an old general store with a saggy wooden porch and old wagon wheels riveted together to make a railing. I would stop there if it was still open, and buy tomatoes and tortillas and cheese. At first the dark buxom shopkeeper regarded me with suspicion, but after the third or fourth visit she was friendlier, and even asked me if I was staying at the bunkhouse.

"Good people, the Valdez family," she said approvingly.

The first weekend there alone was perhaps the greatest silence I had ever heard. People who have lived all their lives in the city don't understand how much noise an open space makes. Even if there were only earth and air, the wind seems to echo simply from moving into valleys and over hills. Then you have the screaming grasshoppers, the chirping squirrels, and dry branches creaking in the woods.

In the evening, when it was too dark to paint, I would light the three kerosene lanterns.

Beneath the couch I found a cardboard box of books. Someone in the family had evidently been a great reader, or perhaps it was a collection pieced together gradually by different workers who had lived there. There was no obvious theme to the collection, mysteries and paperback thrillers lay alongside biographies of Einstein and Alexander Hamilton. There were old, dog-eared classics, Mark Twain and Steinbeck and Proust. The books made me feel at home. I remember my parents reading to me as a child. I don't think they ever really regarded me as a child, but only a small adult; and when they read to me it was not from brightly illustrated children's books, but from whatever they happened to be reading themselves, as if they assumed that being of their blood I must share their intellectual interests. I remember my father's Russian stage, when I was not yet six years old. He read aloud from Tolstoy and Pasternak and Dostoevsky. Wherever he had finished reading himself is where he would begin; so if he had time to read during the day, there might be a fifty-page gap in my night time stories. I don't think this ever bothered me. I don't think I saw the stories or characters as continuous, but rather as dream-like scenes from that other, adult world that I observed with curiosity but without longing. I have read these authors since and the works are vaguely familiar; but the worlds I imagined as a child were built from a child's understanding of the vocabulary. The words I didn't understand were only a kind of soothing background music to my own imagination.

But mostly in the bunkhouse I painted. I worked very quickly, not because I was in a hurry, but because one step led naturally to the next, and I was unaware of time. Over two months I completed four canvases, one more of the Ranchos de Taos church, and three different views of a pelvic bone.

34

There were some days that summer that were normal, where we were like normal people and it was good; when Jake and I would get out of work, and Maya and Omar would be waiting for us, and we would do things that normal people would do, as if we had no secrets from the world or from each other. We'd go down to the park with the pond and feed the ducks stale bread. We'd watch Maya and Jake trying to fly their impossible kite, the one that folded out into a series of cubes in the wind with four strings that they would have to untangle every time.

"If I were a kite I'd only have one string," Omar announced.

"I'd be a rocket ship kite," I said.

"I'd be a dragon kite," he said.

Maya would stand in complete concentration holding the kite, waiting for the wind to be just so, then *go!* she'd yell and Jake would run, letting out the string. And the times the wind would catch the kite they would stand laughing, proud, as if they were the first to ever fly a kite, and I would almost forget.

I remember one time Jake had just gotten the kite up in the air and was triumphant, laughing, *look*, he said, *Maya, look*. But Maya wasn't looking at him, she didn't see him at all, but she was smiling. I followed her gaze and saw a child, probably two years old, being propped up by his mother. He wore a little denim hat and his belly protruded over the top of his pants like a troll. His mother was squatting down and wiping something from the corner of his mouth, but he was gazing over his mother's shoulder, fascinated by Maya. He stared at her the way that babies stare, round-eyed and unjudging. Then, *Maya,* Jake said again, and she looked away.

Sometimes Maya and I would go to the farmer's market alone and not talk about it at all. We'd buy salad greens and tomatoes, and she'd say, *no, no, those apricots are no good, get these,* when I couldn't tell the difference. I couldn't believe they didn't know, Maya about Jake or Jake about Maya, or either of them about me, *how can you not know!* I wanted to scream at them all, *it's right in front of you!* But they didn't know, really.

I asked Maya once, "How can he not know?"

"He doesn't want to know," she said, meaning that Jake was simply incapable of knowing, that the truth would shatter him.

"Would you tell me if he did know?" I asked.

"No, probably not. But he doesn't."

It was the same with Maya, I realized. She couldn't know about me and Jake because she just simply couldn't, because it would destroy her. It was outside of her realm of possibility.

35

When I wasn't painting up north, I worked at the museum. I would see Jake there and pretend that everything was the same as it had ever been. If he noticed that I'd been away more, he didn't ask about it. I'd told him that Omar and I had been spending time at the bunkhouse, and he seemed content with that. From where I sat in the gift shop I could see him framed in the doorway, charming women as he told them they had to leave their handbags at the front, or making groups of school children laugh and happily behave. I would rearrange postcards and dust folio books as if I didn't notice him, but the truth is that every time he moved or smiled I ached.

Jake and Omar shared some of the same genes, but they were fundamentally different. Jake saw people as basically good, with a few bad qualities; Omar saw them as bad, with a few good qualities. Jake's default position was amused, Omar's was defensive. Omar was narrower, the geology of his face more pointed, finer. You saw his cheekbones and the classic hook in his nose. Jake was softer. Not fleshy, but you noticed the muscles of his jaw before the bone, and you saw his thick lips before his rounder nose. Over time, I realized that I saw them always in light of the other—all of Jake's characteristics existed in my mind as complementary to Omar's.

I was drawn to Omar because there is something secret and arrogant in me, too. A part of me and him both perceived the world with utmost seriousness. But Jake was looser, happy-go-luckier. He assumed the best, and the worst rolled easily off of him.

When Jake had said that Maya kept him straight, I realized that she was a totem of stability in his world that pulled and tempted him in so many directions. Though he was older, Jake seemed to be the younger of the two—he reached out for shiny, pretty things. Maya was motherly, in a competent, no-nonsense way. In any situation, she would know what to do. She was a fixer of broken things, an applier of band-aids, a preparer of nutritious meals. I wonder now if Jake's infidelity was no more than the last, dying kick of his rebellious nature, which was being tamed, not unwillingly, by Maya's patient love. Whereas for me, it was perhaps the first womb-kick of a nascent rejection of the control that Maya and Omar were beginning to wield in my life. The affair was an act of mutual rebellion, I tell myself now.

But I don't think that's true. I think we are programmed, despite ourselves, to love love. When one person reaches out a hand in longing, or casts an invitation with her eyes, the other cannot help but respond. We are all born hungry.

36

Then I stopped sleeping. It was too dry. It was too quiet, it was too hot, the streetlight outside my window was too bright. If I stayed with Omar, he was too warm, too noisy, too sprawling. At home, my mattress was too lumpy, sheets too twisted, throat too dry, crickets too loud, Jake too close, Maya too close.

The less I slept at night, the more I slept in the days. I was late for work three days in a row, and Aline pulled me aside to say she was worried about me.

"It's nothing," I told her.

One night I lay awake, studying the flake of paint that was peeling from the corner of my ceiling. I could paint that shape from memory, an abstract line in the shape of a small country, Bolivia, Mozambique. My window gaped open in the warm night. There was no moon.

I heard the window above my own open, and the sound of a body stepping out onto the fire escape. I tried to guess by the creaking of metal whether my fellow insomniac was Maya or Jake. If it were Jake, maybe he would creep down the fire escape into my open window. Maybe I would sleep better next to him. I rolled onto my stomach and pulled the pillow around my head.

I suddenly couldn't breathe, and the noises on the fire escape had settled into quiet. I thrust my sheets aside and padded to the window, looked up through the bars of the fire escape. It was Maya.

"You too," she said when she saw me.

The metal teethed into my feet as I climbed up the stairs to join her. We sat side by side and hung our feet off into the night, as if we were on the bank of a warm flowing river.

"It's your guilty conscience," she told me, but smiled.

The fires had spread to the other side of the Jemez, and we could no longer see flames glowing at night. It would be contained within a week, the firefighters said.

"Do you feel guilty?" I asked.

"No," she said. We were both swinging our legs. Maya's toenails were painted a dark color. Then she said, "Sometimes."

We could be sisters, I thought, four knees sticking out beneath the railing, four feet swinging back and forth. Someone driving by would think we were. Maya had dainty knees.

"Eric is going to wire the money a week from Tuesday," Maya said.

"Have you ever wanted to tell Jake?" I asked.

Maya shook her head slightly. "He's so honest," she said.

I leaned back on my hands and said nothing. The fire escape's sharp metal pushed into my palms.

"You asked me when we started why I wanted to do this," I said.

"And you said you wanted to do something you were good at," said Maya. "I remember."

"But I didn't ask you," I said, realizing that I wasn't even sure what it was that she did. All I knew was that she had taken my paintings, and come back with money. For all I knew, there were a thousand other painters like me, bringing Maya forgeries of de Kooning, Matisse, John Singer Sargent.

"Honestly?" Maya said. I nodded. "For the money."

"But you live so modestly," I said.

"Patience," said Maya. She stopped swinging her legs and lay back on the fire escape. She would get rust on her shirt. She threaded her legs over the lowest bar. There was something childish about the gesture, as if she were on monkey bars.

"I'm going to sit on it for a few years," she said. "Then I'm going to buy a big house on a hill and grow honeysuckle and have a hot tub in the garden. I'm going to have kids and send them to private schools with catered lunches, then private universities with red brick cathedral dormitories."

Maya spoke with the authority of a storyteller. But her words also contained the wistfulness of one whose dream has blurred from overuse. Her dream surprised me for how conventional it was. She was describing my parents, I realized, and the associates of my parents. I'm not sure what I imagined Maya's dreams would be, but had expected more extravagance. Banquets of hummingbird eggs, gardens of flowers that bloom for one day every decade.

I wondered if these would be Jake's children, and how he would feel about the red brick education.

"I'd like to build my own house," I said. "In the desert, with sliding doors I could leave open all day."

The stars were bright and indifferent above us.

37

I asked Omar the same thing one day as we were walking to his apartment from the coffee shop.

"Guilty abour what?" he asked.

"Lying," I said. "There's an arrogance to how we treat the people who are buying this stuff. Really, we're just simple scam artists."

"Come with me," Omar said. He turned left on the next block and walked in the opposite direction from his apartment.

He walked towards Canyon Road, where all the galleries are, choked with browsing tourists. It is all narrow, one-person sidewalks and wide window displays, infested by the legions of the wealthy, shiny SUVs glinting in the sun, rental cars of those visiting from the east.

We walked in silence for awhile, me wondering why he'd come this way. We slowed to squeeze by couples admiring sidewalk sculptures. Occasionally, we would pass a gallery door when someone was coming in or out, and the air-conditioned air would swirl around us into the street. We stopped at the bar towards the end of the street, with a raised patio looking out into the mélange. Omar brought his chair around the table right next to mine, so our shoulders were touching.

"You can feel guilty for some abstract philosophical reason," Omar said finally, when our drinks had arrived and the waitress left. "But don't ever feel guilty on account of the buyer. The buyer," he said unapologetically, "is scum."

"You'll turn me into a misanthropist," I said, trying to turn the conversation light, not really wanting to talk anymore.

"They're the misanthropists," Omar said. I was surprised at his fierceness.

We watched the crowd drift by, a continual sea of wealth, self-conscious in their casual dress, clothes they assumed to be Santa Fe style. Men talking importantly on cell phones.

"These are your customers," Omar said. "They're oil magnates, day traders, CEOs of companies that profit from the suffering of third world countries. Do you think they suffer from guilt?"

We watch them walk in and out of galleries with South-western-themed art. Horses galloping on the plains, manes flapping. Omar's disdain and resentment was palpable, and contagious.

"They don't love O'Keeffe," he said. "They love her fame."

A slanted dirt parking lot across from us, big shiny cars like beetles crawled in, looked vainly for a slot, crawled out again. *It was Rachel's yacht*, said a passerby.

38

Maya wanted to see the paintings I'd been working on, so one Saturday we drove together to the bunkhouse where I kept them. After spending so much time alone in that room, it seemed crowded with two people in it; so I went out and stood on the porch while she looked at the work I'd been doing. It was still painfully dry, and at noon even the birds were quiet. At the edge of the meadow, the pine forest rose like a dark fortress. After awhile Maya came and sat on the porch beside where I stood. She didn't say anything about the paintings, but I knew she liked them.

"I think I envy you," she said.

"Me?" I was genuinely surprised.

"You're young," Maya said. "You're talented, you come from a good family. You're independent." Maya reached for the stem of a tall weedy grass growing by the porch and folded it between her fingers. "You don't seem to need anyone," she said.

"People are always telling me that," I said. The truth is that I have just never met anyone that fulfills the great need that I do have.

"You certainly don't need me," she said. She pulled the grass from the bottom, so all the seeds came free in her hand.

"Did you tell Omar to sleep with me?" I asked.

Maya looked into the looming fortress of trees. "Omar is crazy about you," she said. "I've never seen him care about anyone the way he cares about you."

There were no clouds, but the moon was visible in the day, a bleached-out rock.

"Are you happy?" she asked. "With Omar?"

"I think we understand things about each other," I said carefully.

"Are you happy with the paintings?" she asked.

"I've been discontented since the day I was born," I said.

"You should be proud of them," Maya said. "You should always take pride in competence. Take pride in a thing well done."

"But what if it's a bad thing?" I asked. "What if it's a bad thing well done?"

"It's not," Maya said. "You're bringing O'Keeffe's vision to more people. You're keeping her alive, in a way. The world she saw was so beautiful, Ivy, and you see that world too. And that world didn't have to die when she died. It's a good thing, and one that you're doing well."

I didn't speak, but I sat next to her on the porch, and together we pondered the line where the blonde grass met the forest.

"Hang in there for a few more paintings," she said, finally.

39

That week a man I had never noticed before began coming to the museum regularly. There are hundreds of people that pass through each day, and I'm not sure what it was about this man that made me remember him. Perhaps it was his air of assumed ease. A self-conscious ease, as if he were aware of invisible movie cameras rolling beside him. His shoulders were loose as a sleeping animal's shoulders are, always with the quiet threat of springing awake. He carried nothing and walked with his hands in his pockets.

I first noticed him talking to Jake in the entranceway, nodding and looking to the side of Jake's head. He kept nodding his head after Jake had stopped speaking, as if he were agreeing absolutely with an unseen orator inside his own head. He spoke without gesturing, hands in pockets. I disliked him immediately.

The man came into the gift shop a few days after I'd first seen him. There were two middle-aged ladies in the shop, the kind who visit every museum in a city and buy Christmas presents in August. The man stood with his back to me at first, examining the glassware. When the women left, calendars and posters wrapped, he moved closer, to the card stand. He turned the stand slowly, picking out cards and examining them, then replacing them. The stand creaked with each turn. His hands, I noticed, were very pale. They were weak hands, and did not match his sleeping animal frame. I thought he was the kind of man who, had he been born two centuries earlier, would have died of consumption before reaching his twenties. He was looking at a card of one of Georgia's earlier flower paintings, split down the middle and with layers of petals and leaves.

"Her paintings are so sexual," he observed. His voice matched his hands, high and unconvincing.

"Some people think so," I said.

He replaced the card on the stand, in the wrong place, over a skull card. Then he walked to the other end of the shop. The gift shop is not large, perhaps thirteen feet at its widest point. There is only one door to get out. The man stood by windows where there are blinds we keep down all day. Through them you can make out the figures of people passing on the sidewalk, but from the outside you can't see in the shop at all. The man stood with his back to me, looking out the window with his hands in his pockets. His pants looked expensive, with decisive creases.

"Have you worked here long?" he asked.

"A while," I said.

"Seems like a good place to work."

"I like it."

"Are you a painter?" he asked, still facing the window.

A shadow moved in my peripheral vision. I looked and saw Jake watching me. He smiled and saluted me.

"Aspiring," I said.

The man turned from the window and faced me straight on with watery grey eyes. He was not an ugly man. Probably in his early forties, with a slightly receding hairline that lengthened his otherwise small forehead.

"We're all aspiring, aren't we," he said.

Just then an elderly woman came in looking for a gift for her granddaughter. The man caught my eye as he left, and gave a little nod and a smile. I didn't smile back.

Later that afternoon, Kate came into the shop on her break.

"How was your talk with the inspector?" she asked.

"What?"

"That guy who keeps coming in," she said. "It's obvious that he's looking for something. He's talked to everyone who works here, like he's trying to get information out of us."

Kate was the kind of girl I'd never taken seriously, with her matching sweater sets and manicured nails, but for some reason I trusted her intuition. She was nosy enough to be insightful, and her intentions were always good. She picked through a rack of earrings, and they jingled as they hit one another.

"Have you talked to him?" I asked.

"Just chit chat. How long I've worked here, that kind of thing." Kate selected a pair of earrings with tiny dangling stones and held them by her face, leaning over to look in a mirror.

"I don't think his wedding ring is real," she said as she was leaving.

Alone again, I walked to the card rack where the man had been standing. I turned it until I found the card he had misplaced. I picked it up and looked at it for awhile. Then I put it back where it belonged.

40

There are many ways to look at a painting.

For example, I stood in the gallery that afternoon in front of the blue and white pelvis painting, the one that is only the empty socket hole, and the sky inside. In order, this is what I look at: first the shadow at the top of the bone, the beginning of the passage from bone to sky. Then the second shadow, at the bottom—this is where the bone has dimension, and this is where I would sit if I could crawl into the painting, with my knees tucked up and my back there on that curve, on the right. Then I look at the line on the left, which is a stark division between white and blue. Then I look right at the center of the sky, which is lighter, as if a very wispy cloud, as if the sun.

Here's another way. I squeeze my eyes shut and when I open them again it is a smooth blue river stone on a linen tablecloth. Bone-shadow becomes stone-shadow. I could lift the stone (which is the sky) with two hands and it would leave no mark on the tablecloth.

Here's another way. There is bone and there is sky, there is transient and there is eternal, there is animate and inanimate and once-animate. There is close and far, solid and gas, there is your death and there is eternity, which is infinity, which we cannot understand by itself, which we must frame within the language of the finite.

Or here. Nineteen forty-seven was right after World War II, when humans displayed, once again and not for the last time, their inherent and terrifying capacity for cruelty; how we can be programmed, easily, to become killing machines. Nineteen forty-seven and nobody in the western world could fathom the future. Nineteen forty-seven the eternity of the sky was comforting, the indifference of the sky to man and the indestructibility of sky. Even in Nagasaki, the sky was there in the morning.

Another. It was the year that Georgia turned sixty, which is beyond the illusion of youth. You know you have passed the halfway point of your life, the balance has shifted and now you have more past than future. It was the year after her husband died, and the lines in her painting are stark, and the sky is the past and the future.

41

The last time I saw Jake as more than friends started like all the other times. We drove up to the mountain, and the air smelled of leaves and faintly of smoke from a distant fire. But when we pulled off the road I felt like walking, instead. So we walked, and the path had small sharp stones and foot-bridges over snowmelt trickles that had trickled nearly dry. Everything was bright from the white bark of aspen trees. And Jake told me about how when he was young he got lost in an aspen grove as night was falling, and all the knots in the trunks looked like eyes and he had been terrified. Then he told me about how all the trees were really the same organism and were connected underground by the same root system; and what we think of as different trees are all the same tree, after all.

Then I asked him, "Do you think about me when we're not together?"

"Sure," he said. "I mean, of course."

"What do you think about?" I asked.

"Lots of things," he said. "I think about us, and I think about the things you say, I think about your eyes."

"Do you think about me when you're with Maya?" I asked, and then he was quiet.

We walked some more until we reached a big boulder by the path, and we sat down. I was sweating more than he was, it trickled down my back.

Then I said, "Once you told me you loved Maya," and he knew it was a question even though it didn't sound like one.

"Yeah, I love her," he said.

We sat some more, and watched a chipmunk run up and down a tree and up again.

"Jake," I said, "This isn't fun anymore. This isn't fun for me."

And he said, "Well."

There was another chipmunk now, and they chased each other around and around.

Jake said, "I guess if you're not having fun we should stop."

He was right, and it was like a big empty hole in my chest that was light—not heavy—and hurt in a weightless sort of way, in an empty sort of way.

Then neither of us had much more to say.

42

That Saturday, Omar and I went to see an opera that Maya had given us tickets for. The sun was just beginning to set as we parked the car and walked towards the theater.

"You've been to the opera with your parents," Omar said. "In Boston?"

"A few times," I said.

"You seem like the kind of girl who grew up doing things like that," he said.

His arm was like a vise around me, strong and sinewy and guiding. There were days I felt that I could leave him anytime, that I could say goodbye and step out of his life gracefully, unchanged. Other times, when I was close to him and saw the fine skin of his temples and the faint hollow between his cheekbone and his eye, I would feel a rending in my chest, and know that when I did leave I would be changed in leaving him. I never doubted that I would be the one to leave, maybe because I felt a space between us that I didn't think he felt.

Omar glanced down at me. "What are you thinking?" he asked.

"That I look like the kind of girl who grew up going to the opera," I said. "What does that mean?"

"It's a coolness about you," he said. "You're unimpressed by things. You take them for granted."

"That's not true," I said. I tried to disentangle myself from him, but he drew my shoulders closer as we entered the opera house, and kissed the top of my head standing in line.

The opera house was smaller when it was full of people. It was a skeleton of a building, really, more openings than closings. It was a building that made the desert around it bigger. I walked in with the sense of walking through some archway or tunnel, perhaps a space in one of Georgia's paintings.

I waited on the west patio while Omar was in the restroom. As I spent more time with him, I had come to recognize the angry resentment that Omar felt towards the wealthy. He viewed them with an injured pride, the same dark politeness with which he looked at customers in his café as they deliberated over the menu. I saw it that evening at the opera, the way he looked at people without looking at them, the women in long skirts and long jackets who arrive in foreign cars with wicker baskets in the trunk, who unfold card tables and director's chairs and spread soft salty cheese on thin crackers, who bring two kinds of wine and rinse their glasses fastidiously before repacking the baskets. Omar had eyed them, unsmiling, as we weaved between the gleaming cars of the upper parking lot.

Then a voice at my elbow said, "Hello, again."

It was the man from the museum. He was the same height as I was, and I could see the grey-blonde fringe of his short eyelashes. He held a drink in each hand.

"I saw you standing here looking like a painter, and took the liberty of buying you a drink. Do you like gin and tonic?"

"I'm waiting for my friend," I said.

"Well, I already bought the drink," he said. "So you might as well take it."

The orchestra had begun to tune and warm up. All the instruments playing together randomly reminded me of the insanity of birds at sunset.

The man handed me the drink. His cufflinks were silver and very shiny, shaped like little dice.

"Are you a gambler?" I asked.

"Aspiring," he said. He sipped his drink daintily, and I noticed that he was not wearing his wedding ring. The lights dimmed twice, and I watched the shadow from the bridge of his nose grow over his eye. He took a ticket from his pocket and asked where I was sitting.

Just then Omar strode up between us. He looked at me questioningly, then at the full plastic cup in my hand.

"Omar," I said, "This is . . ."

"John," the man supplied.

"We should sit down," said Omar.

"Look, I'm just two rows away," John announced, comparing his ticket to the ones Omar held. The lights dimmed again, and I left the drink untouched on a wall as we took our seats.

"Who's that?" Omar demanded in a whisper.

I told him I didn't know. "He comes into the museum," I said.

The lights dimmed a final time. The orchestra grew quiet and there was a smattering of applause as the conductor took his stand. I imagined him looking down into the faces of his orchestra. I wondered if Jake sat near the front.

"Didn't your parents teach you not to talk to strange men?" Omar said close to my ear, below the noise of clapping.

"They should've taught me not to talk to strange money-launderers," I said cruelly.

The applause died down and a hush of expectation sat over the audience. I could feel by the stiffness in Omar's shoulder that I had wounded him, but I didn't care. I stared straight ahead.

The stage set was very modern. There were three different colored doorframes poking up in the middle of the stage, like strange plants in a desert. It was twilight, and beyond the stage the hills were turning pink and gold. I hadn't read the program notes and didn't even know if this was a comedy or a tragedy. A woman with mountains of hair was leaning against one of the doorways, and a man watched her from behind another.

Beside me, Omar took a breath as if to speak. Across the theater, thousands of libretto translators lit up red on the backs of the seats. They all changed at the same time, translating the woman's song into prose. I pushed the button by my libretto reader, but it seemed to be broken, and the little screen stayed blank.

"I'm leaving," Omar said. Two rows in front of us, I could make out John's head with its thinning hair. The man on stage began to sing, surprising the woman, and the audience laughed.

"I'm leaving," Omar repeated. "Are you coming with me?"

I kept my gaze forward, on the open and closed doors on the stage. I willed myself to understand what was being sung and did not look at Omar. We were in the middle of the row, and as he pushed his way out I heard the shuffling of feet to make room for him, and general noises of frustration and disapproval from the people he stepped over. Two rows up, John turned his head to see what the distraction was.

I watched the drama play out in incomprehensible song, and thought that this is what I had in common with Omar: we had the same gap between how we lived and how we thought we should be living. For me, it was the gap between the paintings I wanted to make and those I actually did. I wasn't sure what it was for him, but it nagged him and made him sensitive and volatile.

By the intermission I regretted what I'd said, and regretted the empty seat beside me. I wondered if Omar had really left, or if he was waiting for me somewhere near the car. I did not much care about the opera; it was obvious to me that the woman would come to her senses and fall in love with the man, after many passings-through of various doors.

By the entrance gate a fountain splashed, a thin sheet of water cascading over a wall into a clear, blue-tiled pool. Men and women stood and whispered like willows. Twilight was over. A faint blue watercolor washed the western horizon.

I walked away from the opera, towards the tall lights in the parking lot. I walked past the shiny front rows of cars, spots reserved for major donors, to the lower parking lot. It was unpaved and scantily lit. The opera house is isolated, and around the parking lots, dark juniper shrubs spotted the hills. Jake once told me that the original builder had spent days hiking around, shouting and singing to find the place with the best natural acoustics.

I walked up and down the rows of cars, searching for where we'd parked. The heels of my shoes caught and slipped on the stones in the lot. The difference between day and night in the desert is stark. There is no water in the air to hold heat from the day; and when the sun sets, the temperature can drop fifteen degrees in an hour.

There was a gap like a knocked-out tooth in the row of cars where we had parked. I stood for awhile looking at the tire marks in the dirt. I could hear faint strains of music from the auditorium. Crickets. Cars on the highway sounded like whispers. I've never known how to deal with angry people, outer-flame lashing-out people. My parents were rarely angry, and when they were it was not a raised-voice door-slamming angry, but rather a retreat inside themselves. A locked-up-in-the-study-until-it-passes kind of angry. With Omar, I sometimes felt as though I were walking a tightrope.

I headed back towards the glow of the auditorium. I wasn't allowed to return to my seat, but stood in the back looking over the rows of heads, all turned at the same angle. I stayed there after the lights came on, and the audience applauded and stood and gathered coats and blankets, filing out the doors. Then I went to wait for Jake and Maya by the musicians' entrance.

There was one other person in the theater, buttoning his coat. For some reason, I was not surprised to see that it was John.

"What happened to your friend?" he asked. He looked younger in the dim light.

"He left," I said. To my relief, Jake and Maya appeared right away. Jake was carrying Maya's cello case, and she had his violin.

"Hello, John," said Maya, in a voice that was neither friendly nor cool.

"I need a ride," I said.

"Where's Omar?" Maya asked, once we'd gotten to the car.

I told her that he'd gotten mad because John bought me a drink. "He walked out in the first act," I said.

"Temperamental," Maya said calmly. "He'll come by tomorrow and apologize, you'll see."

Jake's hand was on Maya's knee and I had to look away.

I asked Maya how she knew John.

"John?" she glanced at me in the rearview mirror. "He's harmless."

In the backseat, I held Maya's cello on my lap. The case was hard, smooth and white like bone. When we passed under streetlights it lit up and glowed, then was eclipsed again by the swinging shadows of the car. I was reminded of the trips I used to take with my parents, coming home in the evenings after a day hike or a picnic, the remains of our lunch on the seat beside me, fighting to stay awake as the adult conversation in the front seat floated away from me.

"Kate thinks he's a police officer," said Jake.

"Does she?" Maya laughed.

"She thinks he's going after some big art criminal."

"I wish him luck, if that's the case," said Maya.

43

The next day started as clear and cloudless as all the other days in August. It was Sunday and I didn't have to work, so I thought I'd spend the morning trying to paint. After a few hours, my hunger overwhelmed me. I was coming back from buying bread when I ran into Maya, who was just leaving the building. She was wearing lipstick and carrying a shiny red handbag. It must have been just before noon, and the usual midday clouds were just beginning to gather, like leaves floating on still water.

"I'm glad I ran into you," she said. "Come to mass with me."

My stomach was sharp with hunger, and I could smell the bread, with its crisp, hard crust, still warm in the paper bag.

"I didn't know you were religious," I said. "I'm wearing painting clothes."

"It doesn't matter," she said. "Come."

It was quite warm in the sun. Our shadows were small dark puddles beneath us as we walked. Tourists and shoppers crowded the sidewalks. Maya took my arm and we walked in the street, in the gutter.

"I didn't want to say anything last night in front of Jake," she said, "but watch what you say to John Rockworth. I've seen him in New York, at auctions. He's some kind of expert on twentieth-century art, identification and verification. I don't know what he's doing here, but I don't think it's good." She was walking very quickly, holding me close to her side.

"Is he a cop?" I asked.

"Something like that," she said.

Cars skirted around us, slowed by the pedestrians that choked the crosswalks. I wanted to walk under the awning, in the shade, but Maya was impatient with the crowd.

"Maya, how many people are involved in this?" I asked.

"Does it matter?" Maya asked. "It is what it is, and you and I are a small part. Let's keep it that way."

I felt sweat forming on my lower back, near my waistband. My pants had a violent streak of orange paint up the left leg, and I still carried the loaf of bread.

When we reached the cathedral, I followed Maya up the stone steps and dipped my fingers in the holy water, imitating Maya making the sign of the cross. I had known her for nearly a year without knowing she was a churchgoer. I had been to church fewer than ten times in my entire life, and it seemed to me a cold, curious museum. It is lifeless, not a place suitable for prayer. Not dead, but inanimate. Light filtered in the stained-glass windows. Six windows on the left, six on the right, depicting scenes of the crucifixion. In the front of the church, an enormous statue of Jesus hung from a wooden cross, his suffering rendered in red paint on his hands, feet, and forehead. Maya was kneeling behind the pew with her hands clasped in prayer and her eyebrows drawn. She was as earnest as I'd ever seen her. Her lips moved silently. I wondered what she was praying for. I set my bread down on the pew and kneeled beside her.

I do not believe in God and do not know how I would address Him if I did.

I glanced sideways at Maya again. Her forehead was resting on her clasped hands now. I was so hungry I felt nauseous.

There was a heavy knot of anxiety in my stomach, and I suddenly realized that it was a familiar feeling. It was something I had been carrying with me for how long? Five months? I had been preoccupied for so long that I could hardly remember what it was to concentrate. Wherever I was, I was thinking of something else. Every time I sat down and tried to follow my thoughts, I just got lost.

I stood and sat on cue with the rest of the congregation. The church was only two-thirds full, but everyone seemed completely engrossed in the sermon. Except maybe the children, whose feet did not yet touch the floor. They swung their legs and put their fingers up their noses with the same absolute concentration as their adult counterparts contemplated their immortal souls.

People look towards God, yes, for comfort and protection. But even more, I realized, they look to God for reassurance about the mediocrity of their lives. No matter how dull or thankless their weeks are, no matter how many hours in front of computer screens or behind counters, they could take comfort in what God assured them was the uniqueness of their souls. In God's eyes we are righteous or sinners, but never, never mediocre. Which may be why the children swing their legs and pick their noses and are unimpressed, because they do not yet know that fear that defines our adult lives, the fear of being mediocre. Children are nothing but potential and bright futures. This is what I knew, suddenly in church, with Maya beside me biting her lower lip and staring at the pews: it is mediocrity that terrifies us. Not death or aging, but the fear of dying and aging without having done anything extraordinary.

Only instead of praying in hard pews, I had turned to a dead artist. I was petrified by my own mediocre work, and Maya had said, *You could be great.*

Outside the cathedral, the fleecy late-morning clouds had gathered into great thunderheads over the mountains. The western part of the sky was clear. The sky is large enough, I thought, it can sustain the contradictions of storm and sun.

I said, "I don't want to do this anymore."

Maya stopped walking, looked at me briefly, then began walking faster.

"I was so flattered by your attention," I told her. "I wanted to do something great and important." We stopped and sat on a bench in the scanty shade of the afternoon.

"Do you remember when you said that I was keeping Georgia's way of seeing the world alive?" I asked. "Maybe I am, but it's at the expense of my own way."

I might have said more, but I looked over and saw that she was crying behind her sunglasses. I felt my throat constricting. I had never seen her cry before. It was alarming, like seeing one's mother cry.

"I'm sorry," I said. "I'm really sorry."

"It's not that," she said. "Ivy, I'm pregnant."

Everything around me, the manicured grass, wrought-iron fence, leaf shadows, narrowed into a tunnel of surprise. I swallowed. The world slowly re-expanded.

A beetle was trying to crawl up the leg of the bench we were sitting on. His legs couldn't grasp the metal, and he kept sliding back down.

"That's wonderful," I said, finally. "Congratulations."

She shook her head. "Jake's not going to want it."

"He doesn't know?"

Maya was leaning forward now, elbows on knees, her shoulders shaking. I studied the dirt around the legs of the bench. It was a dry patch where the sprinkler didn't reach. The beetle tried again and tipped over backwards, waving his tiny legs in the air.

"How long?" I asked.

"Almost three months," Maya said.

I sat awkwardly as Maya cried. I thought about the new cluster of cells inside of her, dividing and growing from a little blackberry to an amphibious being with its own peanut heart fed by Maya's blood. It made me dizzy.

I didn't know what to do, so I put my arm around her and felt her shaking. The embrace was awkward at first, but she leaned into me and I found myself smelling her hair. It was very soft. I held her there.

"That's not all," she said. "They're going to catch me, I know it."

"No," I said. "Maybe they haven't sold anything yet. We don't have any money yet, right? We can say it was just an exercise. It's not signed, we haven't done anything wrong."

Maya freed her arm from me and wiped her eyes, lifting her sunglasses to the top of her head. She didn't look at me, and I started to feel very cold despite the sun.

I had almost forgotten about the money that Eric was supposed to wire in the past month. I'd asked Maya once, and her response had been distant and noncommittal, she would let me know when the money came. I hadn't asked since.

"They haven't sold yet, have they?" I repeated. As soon as I asked, I knew that they had. Maya winced. I was light-headed. I didn't know if I was feeling hunger or fury or fear. Maya had her eyes closed now, but she was still shaking.

"You didn't tell me?" I asked, my stomach churning. Maya kept her eyes closed, as if trying to shut out the world.

"You've got to be kidding," I said flatly. I simply could not believe that they would plan to keep the money themselves.

"I swear I was about to tell you," she said. "Things are horrible right now."

I said, "This is so easy for you, isn't it? Lie to me, lie to Jake. Your friends are so convenient."

As soon as I said that, I regretted it. There are some words that are too cruel, even if they are truths. Especially if they are truths. Even if Maya had gotten the museum job for Jake in order to have access to the archives, I wished I hadn't spoken.

Maya began to cry again. "I didn't think it would be like this," she said. "I didn't think I would love him like this."

An ant approached the beetle, who had been lying still in the patch of dirt, but began to wave his legs again, with new desperation.

"I messed up, Ivy," Maya said in a flat voice. "I want to have a family with him. I want to be a mom. Not a criminal."

I moved so our legs were touching, and sat, leaning forward with my elbows on my knees. There was nothing more I could say.

A throaty rumble came from the clouds.

"It's going to rain," Maya whispered.

"No, it's not," I said. "That's not how rain smells."

I reached out with a fine twig, and rolled the beetle back onto his legs and watched him waddle into the grass.

I walked with Maya back to the apartment, but didn't go in with her. Instead, I walked out back towards the plaza. Three months ago was almost the same time as when I had gone to the opera house with Jake, when he had come back to my apartment. There was something voracious about all this, I thought, a way we have of eating one another up and being swallowed by the world. I suddenly felt very young and stupid. What did I know about love? For me it was only a great hunger. And it was selfish. Everything I did was selfish. I was the most selfish person I had ever known. Every painting was selfish, it was my way of trying to own a thing, because when you paint it you know it differently from anyone else in the world, and it becomes yours. It is a way of making love for those who are too shy or idealistic. I sat on the curb.

When the first drops came, I didn't notice them. But I'd been wrong about the rain again, and it came finally with all the pent-up fury of two months. It was a fierce and unforgiving rain, with strong, fat, dagger drops that nailed my clothes into me and streamed through my hair. I was too tired to move. I closed my eyes and didn't care about the rain, but listened to it beat upon all surfaces equally. It rattled through leaves and broke on concrete. It knocked on the outside of my skull. This is the sound of water, I thought, and it dripped down my forehead into my eyes off my nose, plastered my shirt to my skin beneath the collarbones. There was nobody else around. The plaza had emptied completely, everyone had gone to cafés or shops or museums, or to their homes. Rivers born of rain churned down the gutters where I had walked a few hours earlier. Rivers around my feet, through my sandals.

Back at my apartment, I showered and put on dry clothes. I had just started boiling water for tea when someone knocked at my door. It was Omar, looking somewhat ashamed of himself. He had come by to apologize, as Maya had predicted, though the previous night seemed so long ago I had almost forgotten.

"I have a bad temper," he said. "I know I do. I'm sorry I left you. It was wrong of me."

"I know you and Maya have the money from Eric," I said.

He looked at me, surprised. I memorized his face at that moment, the thin bump in his nose, the way it came to a sharp V in the end. The whites of his eyes were brilliant compared to the deep black irises. I memorized this, and the curve of his lower lip and the slight asymmetry of his eyebrows. The shadows below his brows and cheekbones, the tight curl of his hair, cut very short above his ears.

I just wanted to be done with the whole thing.

"It's okay, I'm not angry," I said. "I don't care about the money."

Then he pulled me towards him and closed the door with his foot. He had just shaved, and murmured into my ear, *you're too good. You're too good to me.*

We stood like that in the entranceway for awhile. He was stroking the back of my head. I had left my wet clothes on the floor, and I looked at them in the corner over Omar's shoulder. They looked washed out and defeated, slumped in a puddle of water.

The rain had stopped by this time. Omar led me into the main room where my easel stood. He was holding my face in both hands and kissing me. Outside, the clouds had broken up and the sun shone in individual rays over a city darkened by water. Puddles glinted, drops still clung to cars.

"Omar," I said, "I want to be alone."

He drew back, looking hurt. We were standing in one corner of the parallelogram of light slanting in through the window. My hair was still wet, and it dripped down the collar of the sweatshirt I was wearing.

"Okay," he said. "I understand." He looked suddenly guarded, as if a veil had dropped over his face. From the kitchen, the kettle rattled and hissed as the water began to boil.

"No," I said. "I mean in my life right now. I want to be alone in my life." As I said it, I felt sure. Omar didn't move. His hands were still on my shoulders. The kettle began to whistle more urgently, screaming now. I removed Omar's hands from my shoulders and went to turn off the stove. He followed me into the kitchen.

"What are you afraid of?" he asked. With my back to him, I rummaged through a cabinet, looking for a tea bag.

"Why are you afraid of me?" he asked again. "What are you running from?"

"I'm not afraid of you," I said. "I just need to think."

"You've always been distant," he said. "You are a hard woman, Ivy. I should have known. I should have known better." His temper flared and showed itself in his eyes. For the second time that day, there was nothing I could say.

"You know what your problem is," Omar said bitterly, "you're in love with your own loneliness. You isolate yourself and that is your fucking muse."

As he was leaving, he turned and said, "This is the last time you'll see me." He did not slam the door, but pulled it behind him almost gently, with a definitive click.

I stood in one place in my apartment for awhile after he'd left. The clouds slid off to one side of the sky again. They were very dark grey still, but flatter, deflated.

And in my mind, Omar said it again. *You're in love with your loneliness.* He said, *You isolate yourself and that is your fucking muse.*

I thought I should maybe hang up my clothes to dry, but when I walked to the entrance where they still sat in their own puddle, it seemed like an excruciating amount of work. So I went back into the studio and sat on the mattress. I looked out the window and from where I sat on the floor, I could see the swoop of power lines and the tops of the cottonwoods. Presently, a songbird of some kind came and sat on the power line. I had passed beyond hunger now. I thought maybe I should go buy food, but the world had become unbearably large. From the mattress to my door was a dozen miles, and to the street was unfathomable.

I lay down and pulled a blanket over my shoulders. It was small, made of thick, rough wool, and my feet stuck out from the bottom unless I curled into a tight ball. I thought about all the times that Omar had been lying there with me. How attentive he'd been, almost compulsively so. *Is this okay?* He'd ask. *Is this good?* One time, moving above me, he'd said, *I don't want to be needy. But I need you to talk right now.* His voice almost pleading. *What should I say,* I'd asked after a time. *Anything. Please say something.* But I hadn't been able to think of any words.

I must have fallen asleep, because when I opened my eyes the light was dusky. I could just make out the outline of my easel against the wall. The streetlight outside my window cast the same slanted rectangle of light over the floor as the sun had earlier.

I'd been woken up by a noise upstairs, something dropping. I heard raised voices, and then it was quiet again. I rolled onto my other side and pulled the blanket up to my chin.

44

Maya came over the next evening. It was warm, and I had the windows open and fans blowing from the windowsills. Pages from a newspaper on the table rustled in the breeze.

We stood in my kitchen chopping onions and spinach to make omelets. Now that I knew, I looked for signs in her face. Pregnant women are supposed to glow, I thought. She chopped onions carelessly and perfectly. The tip of the knife never left the cutting board, and she cut in an arc around the tip, steady as a snare drum. Onions didn't make her cry.

"I talked to Omar," she said. "He told me."

"It's for the best," I said.

"Are you sure?" she asked.

I was trying to light the stove, but my pilot light had blown out. When I lit a match, the flame roared up for a second, then settled.

"I'm sure," I said.

We worked in silence. Maya didn't say a word about the money, so neither did I. I was tired of fighting, tired of conflict. I wanted my life to be simple and normal again, I wanted to talk of simple and normal things.

I poured oil into the pan, let it heat, and swirled it around evenly. Maya scraped the onions off the cutting board. I watched as they started to sizzle, then became translucent. It was so simple, I thought. We are simple. We cook every day, we eat and we sleep and we work. That is what adults do, I thought. It was enough for everyone else, it could be enough for me. The sound of the fork hitting the sides of the bowl as Maya whisked eggs. She stood with her back to the counter, holding the bowl in front of her. Her belly looked as flat as ever. I put the onions on a separate plate, and watch her pour the eggs into the hot pan.

"Are you going to keep it?" I asked.

Maya put a glass cover over the pan.

"I am," she said, and smiled a smile I hadn't seen before. "I'm going to keep it."

"Have you told?" I asked.

"No," she said. "It doesn't matter."

She lifted the lid and added onions, spinach, cheese. I handed her a spatula and she folded the omelet gently, perfectly, like I never can.

"It matters," she said after awhile, "but my mind is made up."

45

When Georgia was twenty-seven-years old, she knelt on the floor of her bedroom, which was covered by cheap student sketch paper. Charcoal dust coated the palms of her hands, the knees of her black dress.

She said she was tired of painting as she had been taught, painting *what other people paint*.

She had decided to paint the shapes and shadows she saw in her mind. She said she was disgusted with everything she'd ever done, and was glad to be disgusted. She said she would rather never paint again than to spend her life on imitations.

Georgia drew on her hands and knees, with her serious eyes, severe forehead, charcoal on her palms. I look at her, crawling like a man lost in the desert. And think, God, I am in love with this woman.

But my love is always colored by jealousy, it comes from an unwashed palette. Love should be a solid color, I think. White maybe, or deep blue, or maybe a different color for each different love. Loving your parents a buttercup yellow. But Georgia was kneeling for nobody but herself, and my colors come out wrong: they melt into one another, jealousy taints my love, orange streaks in white.

46

Then I didn't see Maya for several days. I went to work in the mornings and came home in the evenings. I walked and read and made sketches. I had more time by myself now that I didn't go to the café or see Omar anymore. I hardly saw Jake, either, as he had rehearsals after work nearly every day. Apparently he had been rotated to a different guard position, because when I looked through the gift shop door now, I only saw Francis, who was stout and ponytailed, with a jaw like a bulldog.

At first this absence did not seem strange, but as the week went on and I still didn't see Maya, I realized how accustomed I'd grown to her small bell voice. I realized that I had never sought her out. We just seemed to run into one another on the stairs or outside the museum or in the café, or she would just come down and knock on my door. I hardly ever made the effort to see her. I never went to their apartment unless specifically invited. Somehow it seemed we'd always just come together; and for the first time, I found myself wondering how much of this had been by Maya's design.

It rained nearly every day now, and each time the sky split anew. The afternoons were wracked by electricity, lightning split like rivers in great jagged bolts, and thunder rolled in two tones. I liked the violence of it, the extremes of brilliant dryness and absolute downpour. There was no uncertainty. After two booming hours of storm, the clouds would be dried up and scattered.

I was walking home one afternoon after a rainstorm, when I heard someone calling my name. It was Jake, behind me on the sidewalk. The storm had ended less than an hour earlier, but the streets were almost dry already, only the water stains in cracks showed evidence of the earlier downpour.

We went to our usual bar, overlooking the plaza. The smell of water hung in the air around the branches, and our seats still had puddles of rain. We dried them with paper napkins before sitting. We ordered our drinks, talked about storms, about how dryness makes static electricity and lightning. Finally he looked straight at me.

"Maya's going to have a kid," he said.

I thought about trying to feign surprise, but instead just nodded.

"When did she tell you?" I asked.

"A few days ago." Jake inhaled audibly, and looked over the plaza to the stone steeple of the cathedral and the mountains behind it. I studied his profile. He wore a thick silver hoop in his right ear, the one that was deaf. I wondered for a moment if the deafness affected his sense of touch, if that lobe were more or less sensitive.

"I told her about us," he said.

I had just taken a sip of beer and suddenly couldn't swallow. I held it in my mouth for a moment, and finally forced it down my throat with some effort.

"I had to," he said. "I think about it a lot."

Below us on the plaza, a small group had gathered around two teenage boys on trick bikes. They spun around, standing on one wheel or another, balancing without handlebars, jumping from the curb.

"I think about it too," I said. "It never should have started."

In the corner of my eye, Jake was still. We both looked at the bikers, the leaves, the drying city, anything but one another. I felt as though I were carrying something very sharp in the back of my throat, perhaps a burr or a small cactus.

"What did she say?" I asked finally.

Jake ran his hands through his shaggy hair, pushing it back, then forward.

"She was upset." He took a breath as if to add something, but then just said the same thing again.

"She was upset," he said.

After awhile, Jake said he thought he'd head home, and I said I thought I might like to walk for a bit. It was early evening. On the sidewalks by the plaza, a few earthworms had pulled themselves out of the waterlogged grass and they stretched, grey and dying, in the puddles. The city seemed quieter after the rain. I found myself walking the familiar route towards Omar's café. It wasn't with the intention of seeing him, it was just the direction my feet took me, the way water always runs downhill.

A leftover raindrop fell from a cottonwood and rolled down my cheek. I had my hands in my pockets and was looking down at my shoes. The right sneaker had the beginnings of a hole above the big toe, and when the shoes got wet, red dye would bleed through the shoe and color my sock.

I felt very light, walking in that early evening. Not in a joyful way, but in a hollow way.

When I reached the café, it was closed. It almost looked like a different building, with the hard wooden door that usually stood wide open behind the screen. All the lights were off and chairs rested upside down on the tables, their legs pointing straight up like stiff dead animals. The only day I had ever known the café to be closed was Christmas. I stood peering into the darkened windows for awhile, as if some explanation would materialize from the interior. The windows reminded me of eye sockets in a skull. Then

I realized another difference in the room. The walls were completely bare. Behind the counter, the huge blackboard menu was still up, and the T-shirts they sold, but my paintings were gone. From the evening light coming in the windows, I could see the hooks where they had been hanging. They cast shadows like wounds.

I walked around the café, past the patio with the cottonwood to the back alley, where Omar had sat smoking when business was slow. It seemed I could still smell a trace of his cigarette smoke mingled with lavender soap. Cigarette butts poked out of the gravel, soggy from the afternoon storm.

Foul smells of restaurant garbage drifted from the green metal dumpster. Coffee grounds, sour milk. One of the lids was gaping open, and a piece of wood angled out. It looked like the kind of balsawood used to stretch canvas. A sense of dread grew in me as I walked closer. I pulled out the wood, shaking off carrot peelings. It was broken and torn, but was obviously one of my paintings. Three painted fingers stretched on the side of the canvas, severed from their hand. The canvas had not been torn but cut, sliced with a sharp knife or razor. It hung in tatters from the misshapen frame. There was something grisly about it, the dismembering of painted bodies. Ribbons of arms, torsos, bare feet. I dropped the broken frame to the ground as one would drop something covered in maggots.

There were five more paintings in the dumpster, splintered and slashed, almost unrecognizable. I pulled them out one by one, shaking off what I could of the garbage. They had evidently been outside for at least a day, and were stained with water and wet coffee grounds. I told myself to stop after the second, but somehow I had to see them all to believe it. The cuts were long and purposeful, each painting slashed five or more times in parallels and crisscrosses. I felt as though I were witnessing the aftermath of an act of great violence.

Once I'd pulled all the paintings out, I wasn't sure what to do with them. I sat down on the stoop. I held my head in both hands, felt the dip of my temples with the heel of my palm. It was getting cooler.

Then I stood up and left the paintings in a broken pile by the dumpster.

There was nothing else I could do.

47

The week passed and I heard nothing from Maya. I began to wonder if I would ever see her again. By this time, everyone in the museum knew that John was investigating something with the local police. The museum director and our manager called a general meeting to discuss the investigation.

The director, Raoul Gallegos, was a smooth-skinned man with graying hair who wore tailored grey trousers and a collarless shirt. He looked as though he would be more comfortable drinking martinis with major donors than addressing the young and attentive staff.

"A fake O'Keeffe has shown up in a New York auction house," he began. "The experts on the case verified it as a fake only because the documentation attesting to the painting's past sales was obviously fake. The painting itself is quite convincing, even to scholars." Raoul scanned his small audience, making eye contact with each of us individually.

"This involves us and other museums in the country," he continued, "because certain details in the framing and edging of the painting indicate that the forger had intimate knowledge of O'Keeffe's work. Almost as if he had access to a museum's photographic archives."

When Raoul paused, the room was unbearably silent. It must be soundproof, I thought. I couldn't even hear the air conditioner. I glanced over at Jake. He looked attentively at Raoul, his mouth serious. When he felt me looking at him, he turned his head slightly and his eyes met mine, but he didn't smile. There is something cruel about being in the same room and so distant from someone.

"We've examined our archives, and they seem to be in order," Raoul said, finally. "We've changed the security codes that allow access to the basement and archive libraries. We have no reason to suspect anyone at this museum, but please cooperate fully with Inspector Rockworth."

"Not, of course, that you need reminding," Aline, our manager said, after Raoul and the others had left the room.

"Do they have suspects?" Kate asked.

"They're not telling me if they do." Aline looked grim.

I'd only recently become a good liar, but I've always been good at silence.

The next day I finished my evening shift a little later than usual. I counted the money in the cash register, straightened up the counter, and switched off the lights. I love being in the museum when nobody else is there; it is like being in an empty church. I walked through the front room with her earlier work, and found myself stopping in front of her white pelvis painting. I can't explain why it captivated me so. It struck me that all her close-up paintings of bones and flowers were like portraits. Each bone and each plant is as unique as a face.

Outside, John Rockworth was leaning against the railing and smoking. I was reminded of Omar in a bizarre way.

"I thought maybe I missed you," he said, exhaling smoke away from me out of the side of his mouth.

"I didn't know you were waiting."

He was dressed tastefully as always, with an expensive-looking watch, and, I noticed, his wedding ring. He tapped his ashes on the railing and watched them fall.

"I was hoping to find Jake," he said. "Doesn't he usually work Mondays?"

"Usually," I said. "I don't know where he is." I wondered how long John would stand there, and how long I was obligated to stand with him.

"You know Jake, don't you?" he asked.

"Of course."

"You're friends?"

I said that we were.

"He's a good guy," John said in a tone that implied that he wasn't so sure. "Honest, hardworking."

"I respect him as much as anyone I know," I said.

John nodded, sighed, took a deep drag on his cigarette. He examined his fingernails as a woman might.

"Yes," he said. I didn't know what was going on in his mind. He took one last drag and ground his cigarette out with his foot. He picked up the butt and threw it in a trash can.

"Well, I won't keep you here any longer," he said, and walked away in the opposite direction.

I walked home past Omar's café. It was still closed and darkened. I decided to go see Maya that night. She would know what had happened to Omar. I should tell her about John's interest in Jake, although she probably already knew. It was early evening and the streets near the plaza were crowded with people. They all seemed to be happy. They were on vacation, they were in love, they wanted nothing but pleasant weather and obedient children. They looked in shop windows and read posted menus. I knew Maya didn't want to see me.

When I knocked on her apartment door, it was not Maya but Jake who answered. He looked at me as though I were a stranger. Evidently he was just leaving, he had a backpack slung over one shoulder.

"You weren't at work," I said. "Rockworth was looking for you."

He had gotten a haircut sometime in the past week. It still hung carelessly in his eyes, but was neater. The cut showed more of the gray hairs around his temples and the back of his head.

"I can't talk," Jake said. "Maya's in the hospital." He closed the door and began fumbling with the key, dropped it, swore, and picked it up.

I was alarmed. "What happened?" I asked.

"They said it's probably a miscarriage." Jake's hands were shaking on the doorknob. "I took her this morning. There was so much blood. I wouldn't have left her, but she wanted me to get her some things. I need to go."

He locked the top bolt with a decisive click. He wasn't looking at me, and at that moment I felt utterly alien from him. His concern for Maya was a mark of adulthood, I realized suddenly. His worry for someone other than himself. Jake with his newly visible gray hairs was an adult; Jake, fallible as he was, loved Maya. It hurt me to see.

"I'm coming, too," I said.

Jake looked at me oddly, as if I were a bizarre animal.

"No," he said. "You're not." Then he turned his attention back to the doorknob, slid the key out and tucked it in his pocket. He didn't look at me again, but ran down the stairs with his backpack jostling his shoulders. I heard his truck start outside with an angry roar.

Miscarriage means that something inside of you dies. Part of Maya had died. Part of Maya and part of Jake was dead in the most real way, in the truest, hardest, most cruel way. Dead in a way that could not be made beautiful.

I leaned up against the wall by Jake and Maya's door, then slid down and let my elbows rest on my knees, hands dangling feebly.

"I'm sorry," I said to the empty hallway. "I'm so sorry."

48

This happened too fast. Too many bad things happened in a row, and they all piled on top of one another and I couldn't understand. I sat in the hall for awhile, thinking about how everyone I knew hated me. Even those who are the most alone among us don't want this.

Then I went to my apartment and didn't know what to do. It was evening—I wondered, what do people do in the evening? Outside it was getting dark, I could see lights coming on in houses across the alley, all the people living the lives I'd promised Omar we'd never live. But what do they do? Why didn't I know what to do? It struck me that our entire lives are spent just filling time. Like a blank canvas, and we're taught to put color from corner to corner, even if the color is white. Not me, though. I couldn't paint anymore and I wouldn't fill my time. I didn't like any colors. I would only sit there, I would not exist anymore. Let the rest of the world exist, I thought, let everyone else fill their time with babies and dinners and seasons, let everyone else feed the ducks and sing their songs and work their jobs, let them strive and try and long and wish and fail and succeed. I refuse. This is my refusal.

I sat and didn't move and outside the birds called to one another, making their flustered preparations for sunset.

49

Maya came home two days later, in the morning. I was leaving for work when Jake's truck pulled up to the sidewalk in front of our building. Maya looked very small in the passenger seat. Part of me wanted to hide, but I stayed where I was in the doorway and held the street level door open for them. They walked very slowly. Maya's arm was linked with Jake's. She was very pale, as pale as I've ever seen anyone. It was how I imagined a dead woman would look. Her lips were as pale as the rest of her face, and shadows gathered like bruises around her eyes. I squinted in the sun as they approached. I was struck by what an ordinary day it was. An ordinary mail truck was already making its way down the block, stopping at each address to deposit electric bills and gardening catalogues and the occasional postcard from Milan.

Jake and Maya seemed to walk towards me for one hundred years without speaking. Maya lifted her gaze to meet mine, and still she did not speak. She said nothing, and her eyes said nothing. They were cold, impassive, blind eyes that did not hate me or even acknowledge me. I wanted to say, *I'm sorry. It's my fault. I'm sorry you lost a small peanut shell baby in a clump of blood. I'm sorry about the house on the hill with honeysuckle. I'm sorry I slept with the man you love.*

I held the door and they passed slowly. I could see the dead white skin at the corners of Maya's mouth. Jake might have tightened his lips into a brief smile, but I couldn't be sure, and he did not look back over his shoulder at me.

I carried Maya's stare around with me all that day. I thought about it as I watched Francis guarding instead of Jake, Francis telling ladies that their large handbags were not allowed and that they must leave their bottled water at the front desk. I thought about Maya's stare as Kate came into the gift shop to ask me if I thought Francis was flirting with her. I thought about it as the mute light from the shaded gift shop windows marched across the carpet, up the wall behind me, over the spines of folio-sized books and glass plates on wooden stands. I was still thinking about the coldness of Maya's stare when I walked back to my apartment, where two police cars were waiting outside, parked behind Jake's truck.

For some reason, I had never seriously considered what would happen if I were caught. At that moment, I realized the risk I'd taken. My understanding of prison was shaped by a smattering of television shows and movies. I would have to share a cell with someone, some stranger. I would be locked away and hidden from society, but my every moment would be public, the company unrelenting. I imagined being in the same place, inside, twenty-three hours each day, and one hour of pre-scripted play time. I would grow soft from lethargy. There would be no light. It was incomprehensible. It was terrifying.

My instinct was to turn around and walk back to the museum, or maybe into the mountains. Then our building door opened, and Maya walked towards me for the second time that day. She only slightly resembled the woman I had seen that morning. Flanked by Inspector Rockworth and two police officers, she looked quiet and resigned, but her chin tilted up proudly. For the second time she met my eyes, across the street, but this time she raised her eyebrows slightly with a look that was almost challenging. Graceful and petite, she stepped into the backseat of the police car as if it were a limousine; elegant and demure, she let the officer close the door as if he were her date. I stood across the street, awkward and gaping, feeling utterly exposed. But nobody except for Maya had seen me, nobody was looking. The two officers slammed their own doors with an efficient clap, and the cars moved away like smooth animals.

I was suddenly very cold and felt very alone. I wanted to see someone who knew me, to be reassured that I was still alive, that my life was still my own. I walked up the apartment stairs two at a time, to the third floor, and knocked on Jake and Maya's door.

"Jake?" I called his name.

From inside the apartment, I heard the strains of a violin. He was playing scales, starting slowly, then playing the same scale faster. I called his name again, and the scales turned to arpeggios, with a loud, aggressive bowing. I knocked louder, one last time, but he ignored me and played on. Jake's world was cracking down the middle, I thought, into pieces that would be irreparable once shattered. I stood outside the locked door for a moment longer, my hands limp at my sides.

Jake played Khachaturian.

I left him alone.

My apartment was unbearable. It was small and oppressive, and I was too alone with Jake upstairs ignoring me. I walked from one end of my room to the other. In the kitchen, I opened the refrigerator door and looked uncomprehendingly at the two squat containers of yogurt and a plastic container of leftover lasagna. Maya was at the police station. Maya was talking to the police. Maya was belligerently silent. Maya was confessing everything. Maya, who hated me.

I could see in my mind each of the four canvases I had up at the bunkhouse. The final rendition I'd done of the church, then a deep blue sky behind the white arch of a pelvic bone, then the same bone view in shades of crimson and yellow, and the most recent bone painting that included a horizon shaped by mountains. I knew exactly where they were in the house, in the spidery shadows behind the staircase leading to the loft. They were damning.

So I left the city as the sun charred the last bit of sky. I was going to destroy the paintings.

The road north was familiar by now. Once I got past the traffic lights, gas stations, and casinos with great floodlights in the parking lots, I turned my high beams on; but they were not enough to cut into the darkness of the freeway, and the night crept lower around me as I drove. I had no music, and I turned the heat up all the way and let the windows down. As if the heat and the wind would chase away Maya's ghost and Jake's ghost. Omar's ghost haunts me too, and I realized I would see him at the bunkhouse, that must be where he is. I would have to tell him that Maya had been caught. He wouldn't want to see me. I was walking into battle.

I was driving faster than I could see, and if a deer or coyote leapt in front of me, I wouldn't see it until it was too late. I wanted to find Omar and forgive the fight. *I'm sorry I lied,* I would say, and he would say, *I'm sorry I wrecked your paintings;* but my stomach still knots when I think of the destroyed canvases behind the café, the precise violence of the cuts.

All I wanted was to paint, since I was twelve that's all I wanted; and I ended up in this spider-tangle, driving too fast on an empty road with nobody I can trust, the world mad at me, without a true painting to my name—only the four awful forgeries that I regretted with all of myself. I don't believe in God, but He says to me, *if you don't trust anyone you will be alone for the rest of your life.*

He puts me on His enormous scale, balancing my sins against the sins of the world. I see that Jake loves Maya. I see this now, saw it in the back of Jake's head and in his hand shaking on the doorknob. I'd seen as Jake laid his hand on Maya's neck and helped her up the stairs that he did love her; but Jake had slipped, into my needy, childish admiration. It had been nothing more than that, a slip, and a slip is not a sin. And I began to hate them both, their complicated and exclusive love to which I was incidental, an inconvenience. Then I thought of Maya, pale from blood loss, and those enormous sin scales shifted and I sank.

The headlights caught ruts and stones in the road I'd never noticed before. The low limbs of fir trees caught in the light, dark silhouettes of trees against a dark sky. Omar is on God's scale too, and he is not pleased to be there. He glowers at me from his God-gold platform, *this is your fault*, Omar says. I say, *you know where the money is*; I tell him in his anger we have to get Maya, we will post her bail.

I am almost at the bunkhouse now, through the aspen grove with all the leaves clapping together like coins ringing. Jake told me that all the different trees were one organism with one root system; and as I get closer, there is no sign of Omar—but I can't believe it, and my headlights pass over the heavy wooden door, still padlocked from the outside. The only vehicle outside is their grandparents' old beat-up truck for farm work, squatting by the empty house, bundles of branches in the truck as they have been all summer.

I don't believe in God, but if I did He would judge me harshly and my sins would loom up over me, a tidal wave tower—and I begin to think of everyone that I've hurt. These are my sins. I want too much: *Gluttony* accuses God, and I say I want everyone to see my paintings and see how special I am and love me, profound and boundless love. *Lust* says God then, *Cowardice* says God, and He is right because I am afraid to try, and I quit before I start, and I lie to people who love me, and I love safely people who can never love me back; and Omar says, *you isolate yourself and that is your fucking muse*, and I'm crying, rivers from my eyes, my eyes are the Rio Grande. *Yes, I love her*, says Jake, and I want to see Omar so he will forgive me, but I will never forgive him and I don't want to see him, and all I really want is to just feel one thing, not one hundred different conflicting things;

it is a war inside me and I would rather feel nothing at all, and just be dead like Maya's baby, which I can see now, a frog-like fetus, fist-sized and slimy with blood and mucus.

My throat constricted and a foul bile rose from my stomach. I stopped the car suddenly, right in front of the house, and stumbled out into the pocked dirt road and bent over, my hands on my knees. I vomited twice.

I have always walked a fine line between arrogance and self-loathing. At this moment, it was loathing. I sank down to the ground, then sat leaning against my front tire, sharp stones poking me. The tire warmed my back, and the car purred and growled like an animal behind me. I don't know how long I sat there, utterly alone.

I knew at that moment that I would never see Omar again.

My face and neck were sweating, clammy in the cold. I felt my heartbeat in my temples.

I'd left the door open and the engine running, and a persistent ding told me to close the door and fasten my seat belt. The car shrank, tiny in the darkness, two impotent headlights and the pitiable insistence of the console light.

I turned off the engine and lights, let the darkness and quiet flood over me. Leaning back in the seat, I stayed in the car. Everything was too hard, it was too much work. I knew I should destroy the paintings right away, but I was too tired. I sat until my eyes had adjusted to the dark and my ears had adjusted to the silence; then I could see the occasional swaying of branches and hear the cold sighs of wind.

50

When I slept, it was hard and dreamless. I opened my eyes the next morning when the sunlight hit my face. I lay on my back in the loft, and watched one thousand particles of dust suspended in the shaft of light from the high window. The dust seemed to glow in the sun, to sparkle.

The panic that had tingled through me the night before had condensed and hardened inside of me. The rest of me existed around that hardness.

I didn't move from the loft, but lay beneath a rough wool blanket. Just by breathing deeply, I could smell that the morning was cold. For a moment I thought of all the things a body does, all the tasks performed at each moment. Fingernails perpetually pushing out from their soft beds, all the glands on my scalp forming and secreting oils, my stomach crying, then satiated, then expelling. It is very diligent, this body. My lungs expanded and vacuumed in air without my remembering. Blood thundered through my atria and ventricles without my even knowing. I had no control, I realized, over the workings of my insides.

I once read a story about a man about to be hanged, whose last words were that he was the happiest he'd ever been in his life. We are anesthetized by time. When we have long futures of sameness stretched out in front of us, we become numb to our days. But when our futures collapse down to a single pinpoint, to a few hours, each minute is suddenly luminous. I swung my legs to the side of the bed.

171

I found a can of chili in the cupboard beneath the aluminum sink. It was as though I was seeing the house for the first time again, the rough handmade shelves and cabinets. I ate the chili straight from the pot, and what I didn't eat I took outside to bury, deep enough to keep animals away. I cleaned the pot ruthlessly, taking great satisfaction in seeing the oil rinse away from the metal.

Then I pulled the paintings out from behind the staircase and considered them. First, I wondered how much money they would be worth if they all sold. The number was high enough that it had no meaning to me. I remembered how I'd felt looking at the first forgery I'd ever done. The inexplicable sadness, as if I'd hurt someone I loved. Looking at these canvases, I remembered painting each of them. Here was a brushstroke I'd made thinking about Jake, about the corner of his lips when he was about to smile. There a shade of orange I mixed after an argument with Omar, the deep umber of our silences. They were good paintings, good forgeries, but I could only see myself in them. I should burn them, I thought, but I waited.

I had missed work, and it was too late to drive to the general store and call. I wondered how long I could stay at the cabin, whether someone would come looking for me or I would slowly go crazy here alone.

I stayed at the bunkhouse that night, and the next night, too. Part of me thought I could stay there all winter, and never go back to Santa Fe. When the snows came, the bunkhouse would be inaccessible except by skis or snowshoes. There was enough food at the house to last a few weeks, but to stay all winter I would have to do some serious planning. I could buy a twenty-pound bag of rice, I thought. I could melt snow for water when the spring froze over.

The only way I can explain these three days now is to say that alone in the mountains, I was in an entirely different world. Everything that had happened in Santa Fe was so far away, it was like remembering my childhood. A book

I barely remembered reading, or a story a stranger had told me. A painting I'd dreamed but never painted.

The woods on the west side of the house were dense and dark with Douglas firs and tall ponderosas. Old trees, weighty branches, they swayed with a slow patience. I walked again a route I had walked many times over the summer, to the spring that Omar showed me. There was no path, but I'd memorized fallen logs, sinewy in their decay. Close to the spring, the trees were sparse and the ground sagged a little. Broad-leaved skunk cabbages cupped the sun. I stopped for a moment by the spring, watched the silt that waved at the bottom as a breeze rustled the surface of the water. Water bugs skidded across the surface, unaware of the winter that tugged at the edges of each day.

A corrugated pipe brings water from the spring to an irrigation pond. Jutting from the west side is a rough wooden dock. Who built the dock and why I don't know, since the pond is not more than one hundred meters across the longest part, and there would be no reason to have a boat. I sat on the edge, and my feet didn't quite reach the silty water. The sun was getting stronger with the day. After awhile, I lay on my back on the splintery dock and looked up at the sky. There were no clouds and no nearby trees. Looking straight up, I couldn't even see the horizon. Just blue, and the only sound the hum of grasshoppers.

I wondered if I was less lonely here than in a city surrounded by people who do not know me and do not care. I think the loneliest a person can be is in the arms of one who does not know them. This is the worst kind of loneliness because it is a kind of failure. It is two people calling to one another in different languages. And then I wondered if it is ever possible to know another person. Or if we are all sentenced to a life of solitary confinement, our bodies discrete prisons.

I undressed and climbed down the wooden ladder into the pond. It was so cold that my breath hitched. I couldn't see my own body beneath my breastbone, because of the dirt and silt in the water. My feet didn't reach the bottom, but I could tell the water down there was colder, it seemed to store all the coldness of the night. So I floated on my back in the sun-warmed water near the top. I took a deep breath and held it as long as I could, staring up into the sky. My ears were submerged, and I only heard the water and the beating of my own heart in my ears. My chest and shoulders buoyed up with air, poking above the surface, and my feet were like weights on the ends of my legs. When a faint breeze came, tiny waves lapped over me. I felt as though I were being carried somewhere, to some end of the pond by the lapping wind, but the sky had no markers besides the sun and I couldn't tell the direction I was being pulled. I let my breath out and my shoulders sank again. I breathed in and out, holding my breath and then exhaling as long as I can.

I have always been a good swimmer, which does me no good in the desert. People who are afraid of water sink by virtue of their own fear. They tense their muscles and fold hard and heavy below the surface.

Then, for some reason, I remembered a time eating dinner at Maya and Jake's apartment—we were all there. It was in the beginning, before Maya had even approached me about the paintings. I don't remember what we were talking about, I just remember that the CD changer clicked and Maya put her fork down suddenly, *doesn't this music just make you want to dance,* she asked, and Jake agreed, *it's dancing music,* he said, and Omar smiled. *No seriously,* she said, *you just have to move,* and we all laughed. Then Maya stood up from the table, she danced not well but honestly. We watched and smiled, she was joyful and relentless, kept moving, her hips figure-eighting, hands over her head. Then Jake stood and joined her, he turned the volume up two notches and we couldn't talk anymore. He took her hand and raised it above their heads, they turned and slid arms over shoulders. Then Omar and I joined them, and we were all dancing not well but honestly. We were young, we were beautiful and all in love with each other and all in love with life, and we were never, ever going to die.

When I got tired of floating, I looked up and found that I had hardly moved at all. I pulled myself back to the dock. My skin was rough with goose bumps and my feet left water stains on the sun-warmed dock.

I did not want to go to prison.

Past the spring, was the grove of aspens where Jake and Omar had carved their initials. I wound through the trees, touching the white trunks. Knots like knobby eyes gazed at me. When I found the tree that Omar showed me, I ran my fingers over the initials. JV. OV. MR.

Standing there tracing my fingers over his memory, a tiny part of me applauded Omar, despite myself. He was the winner, he was the one who got what he wanted. I didn't know where he was, but I suspected that he was beginning a long journey, beginning a long string of buses, trains, and ferries through a continent of brightly colored birds.

I thought about where I would put my initials, with the pocket knife I'd found in the bunkhouse. IW, Ivy Wilkes. Would I like to be next to Omar? On the other side of Jake? Or maybe on a different tree entirely. *It seems so permanent,* I'd said when Omar showed me the tree. *Everyone wants to leave his mark,* Omar had shrugged.

In the end, I left the knife folded in my pocket; and when I left the grove of aspens, it was as if I'd never been. Maybe I don't want to leave my mark on the world, maybe it is enough just to have lived here.

The second night I burned the paintings. They were too big to burn in the stove, so I took them outside to the fire pit I'd cleared earlier in the summer, ringed by stones. First I lay a mound of dry pine needles, then I built a small teepee of twigs. I squatted until my knees hurt, balancing one twig in the fork of another, then building a larger outer teepee. I constructed fortresses of twigs. I built them to burn them down. When the flames grew hot and steady, I put in the first painting, of the church. The paint ran and bled as the fire ate the canvas through at the center first. Flames thrust through the first hole in the painting, making it look as though the church were impaled on a tall dagger of fire. The smoke became thick. It poured into the night and smelled of chemicals, of substances not made for burning.

I burned them one at a time. It was a quiet night outside of the fire. The wind had died down, and it was too cold for crickets. I hugged my coat around me and felt the dark shapes of the trees looming at my back. When the burning was done, I stirred the embers to crush any remnants that would be recognizable as framing. I stayed and watched until each red glowing spark was extinguished, like another eye closing. Above me, the stars were so bright I could almost hear them ringing.

51

The third evening there, I was sitting on the front step leaning my back against the door. I had my eyes closed in the sun, and was watching the red and black spots swirling behind my eyelids. When I opened my eyes, I saw a thick cloud of dust in the distance, churned up by a truck on the road. I watched with a combination of fear and curiosity as it came closer, and the rumble of the engine became audible. The stone step was warm and hard beneath me.

It was Jake, and he was alone. He parked his truck next to my car. He cut the motor and slammed his door shut, and then the silence of the mountains rushed in to where those sounds had been. His left arm was burned slightly darker than the right, from resting it on the window. He wore sunglasses that made him look tough, like a police officer. He looked up at me long enough so that I began to wonder if he was looking at something behind me. Then he lifted his hand in greeting. I returned the tentative gesture.

It had been only a few days since I'd seen him, but it seemed longer.

I love how he slouches a little when he walks, or when he has been standing too long. I love the way he pulls his eyebrows up in the center when he is concentrating. I love how he bites his upper lip when he is listening, how he closes his eyes when he plays the violin. I love how big his hands are. Even if I'm looking the other way, I know when he walks into a room.

I didn't move as he approached me. His boots had licks of dust around the toes. He sat next to me on the step.

"Maya told me about the painting," Jake said. I wasn't looking at his face when he said this, and I didn't see his expression.

"The one she took to New York," he continued, as if I didn't know. "She told me what she did, but she didn't tell me who made the painting."

I nodded to his comment, not wanting to acknowledge what he must have known. We weren't looking at one another, but straight ahead. The sun was still in our faces, but the tree shadows were lengthening and would reach us soon.

"I'm not stupid, Ivy" Jake said, in a voice as hard as I'd ever heard from him. "Was it you?"

Maya had lied for me, and this bewildered me. Was it possible that she would protect me after all that had happened? Maya had lied for me, she would let Jake believe I was innocent, but he knew by looking at me.

"Fucking Christ," he said. "Why?" He stood up, as though he couldn't bear to be close to me, and ran one hand through his hair.

I looked down. My shoelaces were frayed at the ends.

"I wanted to do something important," I said, finally. "Something great."

"The inspector wants to talk to you, which is why I came to get you," Jake said. "Ivy? Are you hearing me? The police are questioning everyone at the museum."

The angle of the sun was blinding. The day was ending, again, and someplace on the other side of the world the day was beginning, and the rising sun was blinding someone else's eyes.

"Did you tell?" I asked.

"I told them the truth," he said, grim. "I thought she liked me for my personality." He laughed a little when he said this and it sounded strange, like a mechanical laugh.

I thought about the day Maya told me she was pregnant. *I didn't think it would be like this*, she'd said. None of us had. No matter how we strategize and plan our lives, it seemed like something always caught us unawares. We are derailed by our desires.

A raven landed on the ground behind Jake's truck and called indignantly to us, then turned its back and spread its tail feathers.

"Did you tell about me?" I asked.

Jake was looking at the raven, too. He hadn't been shaving, and new stubbly hairs grew around the edge of his usually trim beard.

"No," he said. "I didn't say anything," he was shaking his head, as a man who has given up shakes his head. As a man who has lost an argument. Then he came and sat back down beside me.

He said, "Remember I once said I think about us a lot? It's the way you look at me. With such . . . admiration." He paused, and I was a little surprised. I hadn't known it was so obvious.

"It seems like you think so much of me, Ivy. But I'm not sure you know me. I'm not sure I'd live up to your expectations."

Maybe he was right. Maybe I didn't know him, or anyone. I watched the raven strutting back and forth on the wall, turning one foot all the way around and then the other, to change directions. The difference between a raven and a crow is that ravens fly alone.

After a little while I said, "Jake, I know she loves you. I'm sure of it."

"Yeah, but I was real convenient, wasn't I?" he said.

Maya had lied for me. Even after I had betrayed her, she hadn't told that I was the forger. Maya had lied, she would have let Jake believe I was honest.

Then I was crying.

"Christ," Jake said, not unkindly.

"It's my fault," I said. "It's my fault about Maya. She found out what we did and it made her so upset that she miscarried."

Jake looked down at his lap for a moment. He'd taken off his sunglasses and held them in one hand. When he looked at me, his eyes were serious. Brown eyes, not brown-black like Omar's, but almost with a reddish tint, like the coat of a horse.

"That's ridiculous," he said. "If it were true, then it would be my fault and not yours."

He lifted his fingers so they laced through mine. It was comforting, like a parent's touch. "No more crying," he said. And we sat together and were quiet as the shadows rolled closer.

52

The next day I let Jake take me to the police station where John was methodically interviewing all of the museum staff. Jake didn't come inside with me, but waited at the curb in his truck, like a parent dropping a child off at his first day of school. My feet scraped over the concrete steps into the building. They felt like blocks of granite. They were too heavy to run away, even if Jake hadn't been watching.

In a windowless room with a linoleum floor, I sat in a stiff chair. John Rockworth sat across from me, behind a table with a single manila folder on it.

I lied, shamelessly.

Yes, I said, Maya and I were friends. I had no idea, I said, that she was involved in anything illegal. John leaned back in his chair, and regarded me without speaking for at least a minute. He turned his ring around on his finger. I met his gaze, blankly.

"You were . . . romantically involved with Mr. Valdez," he stated, rather than asked.

"Omar?" I said. "Yes."

"Did he ever speak of friends or family connections? Elsewhere in the country or overseas?" I started to pity John. He was a colorless man. I knit my eyebrows together as if in thought.

"He likes birds," I offered.

John sighed voluminously. I felt as though I had stepped into another world, as though I no longer inhabited my own body. I watched myself speaking from a great distance, with an offhand, detached interest in the outcome.

"I'm going to lay my cards on the table, Ms. Wilkes," John said. He told me what I already knew, that the painting at the auction house had been declared a fake because of inconsistencies in the documentation. That on a second examination, experts who had previously verified the painting as genuine saw flaws in its rendering. John told me that Dr. Eric Keppler had pleaded guilty of fraud, and that in his confession he'd pointed to Maya as the source of the forgery.

"What we don't know," John said, "is the identity of the painter himself. Or herself." He stood up and leaned forward on the table, his arms spread wide.

"That is to say," he continued, "we don't *know* the identity of the painter, but we *suspect*. Or maybe we do know, but we can't *prove* it."

I was utterly removed from what was happening. I watched as the new, cool person inhabiting my body spoke. "I'm not sure what you're saying."

"Ms. Rabini," John uttered her name with a note of sarcasm that made my earlier pity evaporate, "claims that she doesn't know the identity of the painter either. She claims that she received the false paintings directly from Mr. Valdez, who has inconveniently vanished."

I addressed John coldly. "Mr. Rockworth," I said. "If you're suggesting that I know the identity of the forger, you are utterly mistaken." My voice issued forth from a steely reserve of cool that I didn't know I had.

When I stepped out of the police station later that afternoon, the air tasted even better than I remembered.

Part III

"There was no one around to look at what I was doing—
no one interested—no one to say anything about
it one way or another. I was alone and singularly
free, working into my own, unknown—
no one to satisfy but myself."

—Georgia O'Keeffe

53

Georgia is twenty-seven-years old. She has put away everything she has ever done.

She will work only in black and white.

She has decided to paint the shapes and shadows she sees in her mind. She says she's disgusted with everything she's ever done. Charcoal smudges take shape beneath her and she wonders if perhaps she is insane.

She draws on her hands and knees, as if in supplication, as if in prayer, as if in humility. As if at the mercy of something larger than herself.

54

I'm taking a break from work. I sit outside and it's cold, so I concentrate on the parts of me that are warm. My back is to the sun. The air smells familiar and I realize that it is fall again, that this was the smell of Santa Fe last fall, dry; and with every changing season you feel somehow as though you've moved backwards in time, that you've returned accidentally to the place you thought you'd left behind. You can get vertigo from the world spinning its seasons around you. It's like being lost in a wilderness and after walking all day—following tree lines, following ridges, looking for cottonwoods that grow near water, following keeping gaining losing elevation—yet at the end of the day you stand with blistered heels and sore knees and find the ring of stones and ash you'd left from last night's fire. That's autumn again. You're just more tired and less sure than the last time you were here.

I pick up a piece of bark that has fallen into this lot. It is many layers stacked together, like a fancy dessert, like baklava that Omar served. I think I'll pull it apart layer by layer, each year of the tree I'll separate and hold, woody, clean, sweet smelling. I'll move backwards in time and it will be gentle and purposeful, a dismantling.

"What are you thinking about?" Jake asks, because he is sitting next to me now.

"Nothing," I say. I hand him the top layer, this year's recent growth. I am giving him back the past year. The bark I hold now grew before I knew him. *He's so innocent,* everyone had said about Jake.

185

He says, "For a week I thought I was going to be a father."

"I know," I say.

"This next spring could have been my kid's first spring," he says.

"I know," I say.

"I'm going to wait for Maya," he says. I say I know, and then he doesn't say how it's changed him, but I know that too. He's his age now.

Around my feet on the ground, I lay the layers of bark I've peeled. Each layer a year, the space between each layer is a bitter winter, and my hands are cold now. I leave it all spread out there when we go inside.

At night I am almost asleep when Jake calls.

"Tell me why you like me," he says.

"I always tell you," I say.

"Tell me again."

"Have you been drinking?" I ask.

I've never seen Jake drink. Ever. I didn't know what happened when an alcoholic drank again. I assumed it was devastating and world-collapsing, but Jake just sounded drunk.

"Because I'm honest, right?" he said. "You said that once." I didn't answer.

"But I'm not going to tell," he said. "I can't tell them about you."

I sit up. "Do you want me to come upstairs?" I ask.

Jake says yes. But then he says no, and hangs up. So I don't.

55

Autumn again, and I stop painting.

At first I try. I sit at the easel, I open my tackle box with brushes and tubes of paint. I wear my painting clothes.

Then I give up and push the easel into a corner, and let a layer of closet-dust cover the tackle box. Maya's trial is scheduled for April, giving the prosecution six months to prepare the case.

The police call Jake to pick up Omar's things from the station, and Jake asks me if I want to go.

"Where do you think he is?" I ask Jake in the car. His heater smells of warm wet wool.

"El Salvador," Jake says. "Costa Rica. Ecuador."

Part of me still wonders if I, too, should run. But to run would be an admission of guilt. If I hide, I will always be hiding. Like Omar is hiding, as he makes his way alone through a string of hostels in Central America. I imagine him crammed on colorful buses with brightly dressed women who cradle market baskets on their laps, sacks of carrots with dirt still clinging to them, chickens bobbing their anxious heads and clucking. Omar would be calm-faced and oblivious, looking through the dust-speckled window, binoculars in his right breast pocket. And part of me is gone with him, as everyone we know takes a part of us.

"It's hard to find a man who loves nobody but himself," Jake says.

In the evidence room at the police station, I see how a man's life can be distilled down to a garbage bag full of clothing and a box full of books, and kitchen tools and dried-up pens. This is everything the police have taken from Omar's abandoned apartment. Everything, anyway, they decided they didn't need. I sort through the box, not sure what I am looking for. Something with his essence, or something that looks as though it has been loved. A strand of hair, even.

Omar's bird books are not among his things, nor is the small moleskin notebook with tiny blue squares where he recorded each bird he saw in his impeccable, slanting handwriting.

I pick up a copy of *The Stranger* that seems to have been read more than once. Creases run down the spine, making wrinkles that stand up like veins. Wherever Omar is, he and I will both be hiding for the rest of our lives. I look at the back cover of the book without reading the words, uncomprehending. Perhaps I should feel angry; but mostly when I think of him, I don't think about the money, but of his cheekbones and his ears and how he watched me. If making love is how we bridge the space between two strangers, what a great space we had to bridge. How the bridge crumbled every time it was built.

I think of my paintings slashed and with rotten food clinging to them. Thinking of that is like touching a bruise.

We build precarious bridges.

I take the book, and we tell the police to give everything else away. Jake drives me home, and we do not speak in the car, both of our minds very far away.

56

Still I do not paint. Maya sits in a cell reading books and waiting for her trial, as defense lawyers investigate all the ways she was taken advantage of by those above her in the operation, the real, hard-nosed criminals who abused her innocence.

In October the days shorten, the days burn brighter and are extinguished more quickly. Cottonwoods and other trees whose names I don't know turn yellow. All the trees here are yellow. They are mustard-yellow and canary-yellow and petal-yellow and dirty-yellow, they are traffic-light-yellow and sunshine-yellow, baby-yellow, golden-yellow, and it makes even the air yellow; and the nights are cold and the birds that are still here sing less and ruffle their feathers defensively. Trees release leaves easily and don't hold on too long or too tight, which would be unseemly.

Then November, and the leaves are on the ground. When the wind blows, they jump into the air like startled brown birds. Only a few still cling to the branches, afraid of heights, or afraid of falling, or afraid of change. November, I wear a hat and a scarf and drive alone to the mountain to look over the city.

On the power line outside my window, the songbirds puff their chests in the morning. They sit evenly spaced on the wire. I should have asked Omar why they sit like that, so exact. When one flits away, the others shift over to fill the space. When another joins, they split and spread again, as even as marks on a ruler.

The first night of snow, I can't sleep. The streetlights reflecting off the white earth make night almost as bright as day, and I stand by my window for hours watching my second winter in this city. Snow swirls around the street-lights like fat white moths. I don't touch the glass, but can feel the cold pushing at the other side as if it were a live animal. We always know that we are going to die, but there are times when we feel our mortality like an extension of our bodies. Most often it is night, most often it is when we are alone, most often it is at the cusp of a new season, as every new winter reminds us of the last one, and nostalgia is surely a symptom of being mortal.

I remember one night I was lying awake on my side, Omar's arm over my ribcage and tight across my chest. From his breathing, I thought he was asleep. But suddenly he said, "We're going to die. We're both going to die."

"Not for a long time," I said. He held my wrist, and I could feel the warm air of his breathing in my hair.

"We're dying right now," he said. He was right.

I don't think Omar was afraid of death, rather he was aware of it always. He never forgot about death in the way that rushed, distracted people forget it. Or the way a man who loves another person forgets that he is going to die. Omar wasn't morose or macabre, but death was a looming judgment on his life, and each day's ending was something lost. He never said as much, but I suspect that when he watched birds preening and cleaning their feathers he envied them, unaware as they are of their own inevitable end.

57

Maya's lawyer calls Jake, but he is not ready to see her, so I am the one who posts her bail. I write a check for Maya's freedom and pen my phone number in at the top. At the police station, I wait in a bare lobby with one desk and one man behind the desk who does not look at me, but at the flat screen of his computer. His hair is black and thinning, his skull peeking through. I could sit in one of three plastic bowl-bottomed chairs, but choose to stand and don't know what to do with my hands. The man behind the desk drinks coffee from a Styrofoam cup.

Standing in the cold police station lobby, I realize that I haven't seen Maya since she was stepping into the police car the afternoon she returned from the hospital. She finally emerges from a slit-windowed door flanked by two police officers, and I get a glimpse of a long, fluorescent-lit hallway before the door silently swings shut. She doesn't seem surprised to see me. Maya's hair has been cut short, and it curls haphazardly above her ears. Newly exposed, her neck looks vulnerable.

She doesn't hug me, but watches impassively as I sign without reading the papers that the bored man places in front of me. She winces slightly as we step outside, as if shocked by the sudden whiteness everywhere. I feel as though I, too, am walking outside for the first time in many months, and the air is clean and cold and wet from last night's snow. We get to the car and I unlock her door first.

"I'm not going to the apartment," Maya says. "I'm going to be staying with one of my students. Turn left here, it's on the other side of town."

I'm surprised, but obey. The silence in the car bristles. Neither of us utters Jake's name, though he is as present in the car as if he were driving. Through Santa Fe in silence, our adopted home, squat brown buildings and grey leafless trees and the blue, blue sky.

"You didn't tell," I say, finally. The snow has already melted from the roads, but the gutters are wedged full of sand-freckled snow, crusted over in bulbous piles pushed aside by plows. Maya continues to gaze out her window, her hands clasped between her knees.

"I'm not protecting you, if that's what you think," she says.

"Inspector Rockworth told me that the bank accounts had almost three million dollars between them," I say.

"Which is evidence against Omar," Maya says. "You're goddamn lucky you have no money trail."

I roll my window down at a stoplight. The air smells of melting snow, and the roads are loud with tires ripping water over asphalt. Wheels fling sand and salt into the underbellies of cars. All the radio stations clamor their joyful beats through open windows of cars and trucks. Ecstatic radio voices outshout one another, announcing mattress sales and grand openings of electronics stores.

"I burned my paintings," I tell her.

The house where Maya's student lives is a modest, single story rectangle with an empty driveway, and snow dripping from the corners of the roof so fast that it is a continuous line of bright reflecting water. At the sound of the car, a flimsy screen door swings outward and a middle-aged woman with blue-black hair and pillowy breasts emerges and stands on the small concrete porch. She raises her hand in greeting.

Maya doesn't wait for me to turn off the engine before she opens her door to exit the car.

"What about your things?" I ask.

"I'll get them later," Maya says. "I don't need much." She starts towards the waiting woman, who is smiling a little apprehensively.

"Maya," I call her back, and she turns. She squints in the brightness of the melting snow. She looks tired, I think, but not defeated. Never defeated.

It occurs to me suddenly that Maya may be my only friend in the city. Perhaps my only friend in the world. Omar and I could have been friends, but we'd never really trusted one another. Maybe Jake and I would be friends one day, but we might not ever completely understand each other.

A trace of impatience scurries across Maya's face as she raises her eyebrows in question. I feel suddenly helpless and impotent looking at my only friend in the snow-melting world.

"I'm sorry," I say finally, lamely.

Maya opens her mouth as if to speak, then closes it. Her shoulders sink a little as she lets her breath out. She shakes her head and smiles slightly, with her mouth closed, but her eyes are smiling, too. Then she turns and walks towards her student who puts an arm around her. The tiny house swallows my only friend, who lets the screen door slam behind her.

58

Days get shorter, and still I do not paint. I wear a wool hat and walk to work five days a week on icy sidewalks. I happily accept my one-year salary increase. The air smells of woodsmoke. The sign for Mazatlan comes down and is replaced by a sign in green cursive reading *Café Esmeralda*. The shop is reopened by an energetic brunette named Erika who hosts open mike nights and serves tuna salad sandwiches with potato chips. I start reading Russian novels. I read Pasternak and Gogol and the short stories of Nabokov. I almost expect something from Omar, a postcard maybe, from the Panama Canal or Costa Rica's surfing beaches. But each day there is nothing in my mailbox except electric bills and insurance reminders.

The earth tilts to its furthest point, is suspended there darkly, then begins its inevitable swing back.

59

One day I bring a cottonwood twig back to my apartment. I think maybe I'll draw it, but I don't. It rests on the bottom lip of my easel. For three days, it sits there. On the fourth day, I pick up a stick of charcoal and look at the twig. It is all knots and bumps.

Art started when the first man drew a line in the dirt outside the first cave, and suddenly there was division. Earth and sky.

Remember the first drawing class you ever took. The ring of faces, the empty chair in the center of the room, awaiting the accused who never comes. *Don't draw the chair*, she said, *draw the space around the chair*. And when you did, you understood.

I put down the charcoal having made only one mark. But the next day I make another, and the day after that, two more. I draw it three times in charcoal and pencil, until I know all its bends, like a navigated river.

When I begin to paint again I approach it tentatively, the way you approach someone who may not remember you. I approach it humbly, and use only small sheets of paper and take pleasure only in lines and shades. I don't try to do anything complete.

When I begin to paint again, it is coming home after a long journey that has changed you. You come home and are surprised by how things haven't changed, but how you have misremembered. How odd it is to put the real life on top of your memories and find they don't quite line up.

This is the world. I am learning to see again.

60

Maya's trial is in the spring, and still nobody has heard from Omar.

Except for the dull, flat carpet, the courtroom reminds me of the church, with half-empty pews. The congregation of sinners.

The lawyers for the prosecution present the jury with copies of the same glossy photographs that I'd worked from, and in turn, members of the jury appear bemused, bored, and distracted. They scratch their noses and gaze at the ceiling as Maya lies. She lies spectacularly.

Yes, she confesses with eyes downcast like the Virgin, she accepted money in exchange for stealing the museum security codes from Jake's files. Yes, she took paintings to the known and convicted art criminal, Eric Keppler, in New York. No, she doesn't know the identity of the forger. Omar Valdez, she lies, with a repentant expression on her face, gave her the forgeries and never disclosed the identity of the painter. She was the willing but ignorant middle man.

The lights above us buzz, and the plastic chair is making my legs go numb.

A bank manager with a broad, sunburned face and furiously shined shoes talks about the account for Mazatlan. Bank records show a transfer of three-hundred-fifty-thousand dollars to a separate account on September 14, and a closure of the account the next day. He is one of several managers at one of several banks; and there is so much money in so many different accounts as to construct an indecipherable maze of funds—and the jury's eyes glaze over, collectively. This is the money from the other two paintings. The ones that were not discovered, and hang now in the private studies of two wealthy collectors.

The lone reporter in the back of the room makes scratching notes on a pad of green lined paper. Then Jake speaks, and he looks at neither Maya nor me. I watch him over the rows of nodding heads, and it seems as though he is one hundred miles away. He never suspected that his girlfriend was involved in anything remotely illegal, he says. It is certainly possible that she would have access to the security codes through him, he says. He has had no contact with his cousin in nearly eight months, he says. His cousin never said anything to him to hint at the identity of the painter, he says.

I think, because of me, this man is less honest than he was before. If I regret anything, this is it.

When I get back to the car after the trial, it is warm from the sun, although the air outside is cool. The prison stands alone in an enormous lot, a plain, walled rectangle in an expanse of dirt with a few patches of brown, optimistic weeds. It would be disheartening, except it is cradled in the great blue bowl of the New Mexico sky. The sky is so big and round that it reminds you the earth is just a ball, surrounded by air, spinning circles around the sun.

Sunlight glints off the cars on the interstate. Instead of heading back towards the plaza, I head south, away from the city. I want to see the train yard. I've seen great rows of boxcars moving across the desert. From a distance they crawl like silent, inching millipedes, but closer up they roar and move too quickly for your eye to follow.

The road leading to the train station is so narrow that there are no lines painted. It is spring, butterfly season. There are flocks of them, white and erratic, flying everywhere in clouds. They are too thick to drive between. I feel a small pang for each butterfly I kill.

Across from the station a general store sits like an elderly man, with a saggy wooden porch and spare shelves lined with aspirin, beef jerky, cans of beans. The rocky dirt in front is a faint red.

The train station is a small adobe building. It is an anachronism of a train station, untouched for thirty years and hardly used by anyone. Most of the trains that go by do not even stop, as they carry no passengers, but only coal and steel and heavy, manly things. There is hardly anyone else in the station, only a woman in a blue uniform coat who sits behind a small window for four hours a day, three days a week. On the walls are framed maps that are fading with age, so you can only vaguely make out county lines and train routes.

The light is blinding.

In the distance, mountains are steep and blue in the light. The station is a pale pink adobe, and the patio is rough and brick, painted with a severe yellow line where one is not supposed to cross onto the rails. There are four sets of tracks, and the rails feel hard and heavy through the soles of my shoes. I step over the oil-stained wooden ties, over the first set of rails, over the second set of rails. On the third set of rails, I begin to walk towards the mountains. At first I have my arms out for balance, but then I don't need them anymore, and walk heel to toe.

I am very alone, in the cool air and brilliant sunlight. There is a penny alongside the tracks, flattened and glinting. A souvenir placed on the rails by a child who either forgot it or couldn't find it in the loose rocks.

The air here is so clean.

The mountains are as distant as a dream, and I wonder how long I would have to walk to reach them, how thirsty I would be, or if I would find someone to give me water.

A faint rattle shakes the tracks through my soles, and I hear a train whistle cut through the wind, miles away.

I squint and shade my eyes with my hand and see the tiny pinprick of the engine light moving towards me like a star in the daytime, its brilliance dwarfed by the sun. I put my arms out to find my balance again. How fast do trains go, I wonder. Fifty, seventy miles an hour? If it were five miles away, how long would it take to reach me? There is a gentle curve in the track and I can make out the cars, black cylinder cars and boxy open-topped cars in dirty reds and blues.

I think about how badly Maya had wanted the baby, how excited and nervous she had been about bringing another life into a world already teeming with lives.

The shaking grows stronger. I can tell it isn't a passenger train, and the whistle is louder now.

One day in 1929, Georgia stepped from a train in New Mexico and the first thing she saw was the sky. Constant and cloudless. She was older then than I am now. She had quit painting and started again, and fallen in love and questioned love. Georgia loved a land as much as a person. There were years she painted nothing and years she hated everything she did. And I am not Georgia.

I step off the rails and watch the train go screaming past, and feel the wind made by pure speed. I try to count the cars but lose track after five. When the last car passes, I watch until it disappears into the horizon, into the vanishing point where all lines converge.